G-Strings

D0886282

New *X Rated* titles from *X Libris*:

The *X Libris* series:

G-Strings

Stephanie Ash

An *X Libris* Book

First published in Great Britain as *Blue Notes*
in 1997 by X Libris

A CIP catalogue record for this book
is available from the British Library.

ISBN 0 7515 3034 4

Typeset by
Derek Doyle & Associates, Liverpool
Printed and bound in Great Britain by
Clays Ltd, St Ives plc

X Libris
A Division of
Little, Brown and Company (UK)
Brettenham House
Lancaster Place
London WC2E 7EN

To Simon Stevens.
An officer, a gentleman and a warm Kit Kat.

Chapter One

'HI. IS THAT room service? Yeah? This is Amelia Ashton in the penthouse suite. "*The* Amelia"? That's right. Thank you very much. I'm glad you enjoyed it. Signed photo? No problem. To your kids? Gavin and Hayley. That has an "e" in it, right? OK. Yeah. I'm calling because my sheets need changing. No, no. They were absolutely fine. I just had a bit of a sweaty night last night. Fever?' Amelia grinned. 'Yeah, I guess you could say that. No, I don't need any aspirin. Just the new sheets. Can you make sure that somebody does that? I'll be going out in about fifteen minutes, for lunch. If it could be done by the time I come back I'd be very, very grateful. Thank you very much. Goodbye.'

Amelia Ashton, famous enough to be known as plain old 'Amelia' to her fans, smiled as she replaced the telephone receiver in its shiny gilt cradle. She was sitting at her dressing-table with its mirror surrounded by bulbs. A real Hollywood mirror of the kind that she had always known she would one day have. Now it was a fixture at every hotel she stayed in on tour, preceding her on the crew bus, to be set up and plugged in ready for when she arrived. It had been a present from her best friend, Karis, to celebrate the phenomenal success of Amelia's very first album and acknowledge that after all those years of trying and crying she had finally become a star.

Amelia studied her reflection. She had hardly slept a wink but, that considering, she really didn't look too bad at all. The new exercise regime she had recently adopted seemed to be working. She had never had so much energy before, though it was a bit of a bore having to take a jog with Frankenstein's monster in tow. 'Frankenstein's monster' was the highly appropriate nickname of Amelia's bodyguard, Franklin, employed on the orders of Amelia's manager, Rowena, after some crazy fan had managed to get into Amelia's hotel bedroom in Chicago and steal two dozen pairs of her specially monogrammed ivory silk French knickers. Amelia had protested at the time that she didn't really mind; after all, she had lost three pairs of knickers to a phantom laundry snatcher in Kentish Town in the days before she got her multi-million-pound record deal. Now she could afford to replace her underwear two hundred times a day if she had to. She didn't want this one incident to mean that she had to have some great oaf following two steps behind her 'for security' for the rest of her life. But Rowena had insisted. You could never be too careful. And after all, Amelia was her record company's most valuable product.

Amelia picked up her soft-bristled Mason and Pearson brush and carefully parted her long red hair on one side. It shone with the polish of hundreds of pounds worth of attention but, to Amelia that morning, even her crowning glory was becoming something of an encumbrance. She wanted to take a pair of scissors to it, have the kind of hair that didn't get tied up in knots or end up halfway down her throat every time she gave a blow-job . . . but Rowena was just as firm about Amelia's hair as she had been about the bodyguard. It was part of Amelia's image. Her fans had paid for that red hair. At the very least, there was no way she could change her look before the end of this tour. Amelia had long red hair on the album cover and that was what her fans expected to see. Who did she think she was, wanting to get her hair cut off? Madonna? That had hurt.

Amelia coloured in her lips with the browny orange lipstick that suited her best. Boring, boring, boring. She had been wearing this lipstick since a particularly successful photo session in 1995. But again, there was no question of changing the familiar cupid's bow, just as there was no question of her walking out of that hotel suite with no lipstick on at all. And the clothes, the clothes she had to wear! Always having to dress like she was going to the opera even when she was only going down the road to get her toenails done. She practically had to wear a full face mask when she went jogging so that no one with a camera would catch the girl who had won the 'Britain's Best-dressed Woman' award for the past two years in anything less alluring than Armani.

Well, Amelia had finally had enough. She took a flimsy paper tissue from the pink box on her dressing-table and wiped the lipstick that she had just applied so carefully straight back off again. Then she scraped her thick red hair back into a ponytail and stepped out of her Chinese silk dressing-gown and into a pair of old blue jeans. She dragged a dirty white T-shirt over her head and topped the lot off with a battered, oil-stained denim jacket that was hanging from a post at the end of her bed. Then she pulled on the trainers that were strictly forbidden outside the gym.

'Reclaim your life, Amelia,' she said in a sexy whisper to the new improved reflection which winked back at her from the mirror surrounded by bulbs.

There was a knock at the door.

It was probably room service.

Amelia grabbed a handful of credit cards and opened the door to the maid as she walked on out into the lobby.

The sound of the Hoover woke the poor young male model who had been left naked and firmly tied to the corners of the four-poster bed.

Chapter Two

'*I CAN'T BELIEVE* you did that!' Rowena was shrieking.

Amelia held her mobile phone away from her ear and casually stirred her cappuccino until the chocolate powder on top of the froth had all but dissolved.

'The maid went straight to the press, of course,' Rowena continued. 'There will be photographs all over the place. Whatever were you thinking of? You were seen leaving the hotel wearing his clothes, for goodness sake! Do you want to send your career into a nosedive, or what? You are not the Rolling Stones, Amelia. You have a certain kind of image. Grandmothers buy your records for eleven-year-old boys.'

'But . . . I . . .' Amelia tried to get a word in but Rowena was unstoppable.

'How I am going to get you out of this one, I just do not know. Where the hell are you, anyway? You have a rehearsal in fifteen minutes.'

'I'm at a friend's place,' Amelia lied. She looked

out through the grimy café window onto the busy New York street. Outside, it was a normal Monday morning. People rushed by the café on their way to work with no care for the red-haired girl who nursed her coffee and a mobile phone. They had jobs to go to. Jobs where they would sit in front of a computer screen all day, filing forms and typing letters and wondering what it would be like to be famous. What it would be like to be rich and glamorous. What it would be like to have a fleet of fast cars at your disposal and a walk-in wardrobe the size of their whole apartment. What it would be like to be public property. Yeah, thought Amelia bitterly. That was what she was these days . . . public property. Unable to kiss a male friend in the street for fear of provoking a scandal. Unable to change her hair without prompting an opinion poll in the national press. Unable even to go outside the hotel in her jeans. It was a nightmare. That was what it was like to be famous.

'Which friend?' Rowena persisted.

'No one you know.'

'Amelia!' The pitch rose uncontrollably again. 'You're not supposed to be with anyone I don't know! Tell me where you are at once and I'll send Franklin straight down with the car.'

'Don't send him anywhere near me, Rowena,' Amelia growled. 'If you really must know what I'm up to the whole time, I'm actually all on my own. I'm having a quiet coffee in a little café on Houston. There's nobody in here but me and the Italian mamma who made the cappuccino, and I'm wearing a baseball cap over my hair so that

6

even if someone were to look at me twice in this outfit, they would not know who I am. I'll meet you at the hotel for lunch in an hour or so, but for now, I just need a little space.'

'But I . . .'

Amelia turned off her mobile before Rowena could protest once more. At that exact moment, the woman behind the counter turned on her battered old radio and tuned it in.

'If you don't love me, I don't know what I'll do . . .'

Amelia winced at the sound of her own voice. It was definitely time to go. She drained her cup double quick, left a five-dollar note to cover the bill, and raced out onto the busy street.

As she wandered back to the hotel through early morning SoHo, Amelia couldn't help smiling at the thought of the guy she had left tied to her bed for the chambermaid to tidy up that morning. A bit embarrassing for the poor girl, no doubt, but better than finding a pile of sick, Amelia supposed.

The unfortunate boy's name was Guido. Amelia seemed to remember that he had been at last night's show. She had spotted him a couple of times as he stood right at the front of the crowd waving a white rose like the one she had fondled on her album cover as he desperately tried to catch her attention. Afterwards, he had somehow managed to get past dozy old Frankie and appeared in the specially cleared hotel bar where Amelia and her crew had gone to get a good-night drink. He seemed to know one of the backing singers – the tall black girl called Darleesa who had once been on the cover of Italian *Vogue*. When Rowena had finally finished delivering the rest of the week's itinerary to Amelia's more sober band members and gone off to bed, Amelia had made a beeline for Darleesa's chatty little party to find out more about the pretty young guy in the tight white T-shirt.

As she walked straight towards him, Guido looked like a puppy about to get his first lick of a really big bone.

'I'm Guido,' he said, as deeply as he could.

'Amelia,' said Amelia, extending her elegant hand. As if she really needed to introduce herself at a gathering in her own honour. 'But that's enough about me,' she murmured as she slid like a cat onto the leather sofa beside him. 'Tell me about you.'

Guido was a model, he began in faltering English full of American affectations. To Amelia, entranced by his classical good looks, that news didn't come as such a surprise. Guido had started out in his native Italy. Done quite a few good shows in Milan. He had come to New York to model the autumn collections. The younger designers liked him for his brooding Byronic look . . .

As he spoke, Guido struck poses. It seemed as though he was constantly shifting so that Amelia only ever saw his best side. But he didn't always want to be a model, of course, he told her later on. He was taking acting lessons too and by this time next year he hoped to be in LA.

'Yes, I can see you on the big screen,' Amelia

told him, her eyes drifting over his smooth full lips. 'And the casting couch.'

One by one, the chattering group around them had drifted off to their respective rooms until Amelia and Guido were the only people apart from the barman left in the specially open bar. Guido was rolling yet another cigarette on the low purple table between them. His hands were shaking and it was taking him a painfully long time.

Amelia fought the urge to reach out and take a handful of his thick curly hair and hold it out of the way so that she could see his face and draw him near to kiss her.

'Do you want one of these?' she had asked as she offered him her packet of Marlboro Lights. 'Only you seem to be struggling with that roll-up and I don't know about you but I would really like to get to bed before daybreak.'

Guido looked up from the table and blushed.

'Would you like to get to bed soon, too?' she asked him straightforwardly, fixing her gaze on his light brown eyes.

He gulped. His Adam's apple moved up and down nervously. He let the rolling paper unfurl itself a final time.

'Let's go upstairs,' Amelia continued. 'Yes?'

Amelia stood up and offered Guido her hand. He shoved the cigarette-rolling paraphernalia haphazardly back in its box and leapt up to follow her. As he did so he knocked the table flying and sent the remains of a couple of discarded drinks all over his scruffy trousers – the very borrowed jeans which Amelia now noticed were embarrassingly stained as she waited at the edge of a road for the lights to change to red.

But the night before, Amelia had just laughed and lightly brushed an affectionate hand over Guido's crotch. 'You'll just have to change out of those wet things,' she told him. This time he blushed deep crimson and Amelia was sure she felt the faintest twitch of arousal beneath the well-worn denim.

They left the bar.

Amelia passed the barman a hundred-dollar bill for his discretion and then she and Guido took the lift which went directly from the bar to the penthouse suite without stopping at any other floor. At the penthouse, the lift door opened straight onto the huge sitting-room with its magnificent view of Central Park below. The room had windows on three sides and when Amelia turned the lights on, the glass reflected the room inside, making it appear even bigger than it was. Three huge sofas and a chaise-longue fitted easily into the central space around a hideously expensive oriental carpet that was complemented by a number-one album's worth of antique porcelain.

Amelia stole a glimpse at her reflection in one of the windows as she stalked across the room and arranged herself gracefully on the petrol-coloured chaise-longue. Guido remained in the centre of the carpet, unsure what to do with himself. He was still trying to take in the reality of his luck. He was actually there. In *Amelia's* penthouse suite. He rubbed the back of his strong neck nervously and flicked his thick fringe back from his heavily lashed brown eyes. Please God, he begged, don't let me cock this one up.

'Fetch me a drink, could you?' Amelia nodded in the direction of the barely used kitchen. 'There's vodka and tonic in the fridge. And ice. I like it half and half. Make yourself one too, of course. And dim the lights on your way back.'

Guido disappeared more keenly than any of the hotel staff to do as she had asked.

As she waited, Amelia closed her eyes and stretched out like a big cat in her tight black bodysuit. She let her high-heeled suede shoes drop one after the other to the polished wooden floor and flexed her toes. She was ready for this man. She had been feeling desperately horny all evening. The show had gone magnificently well. The capacity audience had kept her on the stage with encores for at least three-quarters of an hour over time. Afterwards, Rowena had assured her that the merchandise had practically flown out of the lobby. She said that Amelia was easily the most bankable artist that Midnight Records had ever handled. Bar none. The feeling that hearing that news gave Amelia was almost as good as an orgasm . . . But only almost.

A crash from the kitchen. Guido had dropped a glass. He was so nervous, Amelia reflected with a smile. This was going to be so easy. Why was it always so easy?

'Sorry,' he called.

'Leave it,' replied Amelia. 'The maid can clear it up tomorrow. Use another glass and come straight out to me. I feel like I've been waiting for you forever.'

When Guido appeared seconds later with the drinks he had a big wet patch down the front of his T-shirt that matched the soggy stains on his jeans.

Amelia stifled a giggle. 'You're not having much luck, are you?' she said. 'You can take it off if you like.' Guido put the drinks down onto a table and wriggled the T-shirt off over his head. His naked chest was broader than Amelia had expected, and browner. Sweat glistened in the shallow valley between his tight pectoral muscles. Was it just the heat, or nerves? Guido balled the wet T-shirt up in his hands and used it to wipe the sweat from his forehead.

'Too hot for you?' Amelia asked, reaching behind her to switch on a well-placed fan which blew her hair gracefully away from her face but whose breeze probably didn't reach Guido at all.

Guido blushed even redder than before, a blush which spread down onto the magnificent chest. He shifted his weight from hip to hip and unconsciously (perhaps) found himself in a position which showed his sculptured torso off to even greater advantage. He was like something an Ancient Greek might have dreamed up from a massive block of stone.

Amelia licked her dry lips. 'Come here,' she purred. 'I'm thirsty.'

Guido handed Amelia the tumbler he had filled for her and perched precariously on the edge of the couch. Amelia touched the ice-cold glass to his chest, making him arch his back in surprise. He was very well defined. Very firm. Across his pectorals there was a delicate fuzz of curly black hair. Barely there at all. Just as he was perhaps barely twenty.

'Is that cold?' Amelia asked rhetorically as she rolled the glass back and forth across his chest, leaving a wet slick of icy water in its wake as she did so. Guido had closed his eyes and was biting his full pink lower lip. Amelia wondered whether he was just pretending to feel pleasure as he had been pretending to be sophisticated in the bar. But no. She let her free hand wander casually across the front of his tight, blue jeans. Beneath the zipper she could definitely feel the beginnings of an erection. This time Guido wasn't pretending at all.

Amelia stopped rolling the glass and took a drink. The vodka and tonic, mixed with just a little too much vodka, wetted her full lips, making them more shiny, more inviting. She passed a hand across Guido's stubbly cheek, following the line of his high, fine cheekbones down to the corner of his very slightly open mouth. Then she cupped his chin. 'Kiss me,' she commanded, stroking his beautiful jaw. 'Why don't you kiss me now?'

As if he was about to kiss a woman for the very first time, Guido leaned towards her infinitely slowly. Amelia counted the number of breaths she took before their lips finally met. One, two, three. Contact. The softest brush. His crimson lips were lighter than the wings of a passing butterfly.

He sat back, his eyes wide as if he was startled, starstruck by what he had just done.

Amelia frowned.

'Call that a kiss?' she teased.

Then, all of a sudden, Guido had taken control.

This time, it was he who took her head in his hands, with his fingers twisted through her hair, and pulled her harder against him. And this time, his tongue was immediately between her lips, probing the inside of her mouth and forcing out her breath. Now, when he let her go for a minute, Amelia gasped for air like someone who had been held under water. She wiped her mouth with the back of her hand, half expecting to find that such a forceful kiss had drawn blood.

'Wow,' she murmured, momentarily lost for words. 'That's better.'

She took the opportunity to quickly put her glass on the floor before she spilled the drink all over the place. It was a good thing too because as soon as she had righted herself again, Guido took her by the shoulders and gently pushed her down onto the chaise-longue. Then he climbed on top of her and began to kiss her once more. Amelia automatically parted her legs around his strong hips and sighed with delight at the sudden gentle pressure of his denim-covered pelvis against hers. His nervousness seemed to have completely disappeared.

Guido traced the outline of her lips with his tongue. As Amelia had expected while looking at them longingly in the bar downstairs, Guido's full lips were as soft as any woman's. On his breath, she could taste the mingled aromas of tobacco and alcohol. The scent of some fresh-smelling aftershave that she thought she vaguely recognised drifted up between them as she kissed his chin and the dormant fragrance was released by the heat of her lips. Such a well-kept man, she smiled to herself. That was the great thing about models. The musicians she had taken to bed had tended on the whole to be rather wasted and unkempt, but models – it was their job to look good all the time and this one most definitely did. Amelia happily nuzzled her face into Guido's freshly washed hair.

Guido's hands moved slowly over her body, tracing the outline of her narrow waist through the tightly clinging catsuit. One hand moved steadily up towards her breasts, almost, but not quite, cupping one of the full twin orbs. Amelia sighed with anticipation and then disappointment as the hand moved downwards again. With one hand on each side of her waist, Guido began to rock his pelvis slowly against hers as they kissed. The swelling in his crotch had quickly become a full blown hard-on which longed to be released. Amelia reached down towards his flies to help it out, but her hand was quickly removed and held out of the way in Guido's strong but gentle grip.

'But I . . .' she protested.

'Not yet,' he told her. 'You 'ave to wait.'

For a moment their eyes met. Guido had completely lost his shyness now and his hazel eyes were raised at the corners by the cutest of wicked-boy smiles. Amelia let herself melt into them for the time being, unable to stop herself from giving a little nervous laugh. It was nice to lose control.

Guido's fingers toyed teasingly with the silky tassel that was attached to Amelia's zip. The zip that travelled the length of her body from the high turtleneck almost to the mound of her pussy. The pussy which even now was forcing itself upwards against Guido's incarcerated shaft. With her free hand, Amelia brushed softly across his bottom then down towards the crease where the buttocks meet the top of the legs. He wasn't wearing anything beneath those jeans, she was sure of it. And now, as Guido began to tug her own zip gently down, she laughed softly as she remembered that he wasn't the only one who hadn't bothered with underwear that day.

Holding the zip between thumb and forefinger, Guido revealed only her throat at first, before dropping his head to kiss the triangle of soft white flesh he had exposed. Instinctively, Amelia raised her long hair from his way and twisted so that even more of her throat met his lips. His hips, meanwhile, ground down against her aching mons and she let out an involuntary gasp at the delightful pressure.

The zip was tugged a little lower still.

As Guido planted a single kiss on her breastbone, Amelia felt her clitoris begin to throb silently and was sure that she could already feel the wetness gathering between her legs. So much so that she felt it must be about to seep through the fine silk knit of the catsuit. Once again, she tried to reach for Guido's flies and once again, to her irritation, her hand was pushed away.

Guido had pulled the zip almost to her belly button. Now he sat astride her and carefully eased the fabric off her shoulders, covering them with kisses before rolling the catsuit down further. He worked agonisingly slowly – such a consummate tease – until finally he had uncovered her breasts.

A smile spread quickly across his lips. Amelia arched her back subconsciously to give him her own best angle.

Guido shuffled a little way backwards so that when he dipped his head to her body this time, his lips met with her left nipple straight away. The tiny pink dome was already swelling to meet him. Guido traced a circle around it with his hard, pointed tongue, pushing down into the soft pale flesh with enough force to make her sigh.

'Yes,' Amelia hissed. 'That's nice.'

Guido moved across to the other nipple. It was already erect and he took it straight between his teeth, gently nipping and squeezing the aching bud until she almost cried out on the edge of pain.

'That hurt?' he asked, though his voice seemed barely concerned.

'No,' she sighed, arching her body towards him, pushing her breasts up towards his mouth again. Guido flicked his tongue out like a snake tasting the warm scent of her skin and Amelia groaned as he withdrew his mouth from her, while at the same time increasing the pressure of his lower body on her longing mound as he moved to finish unwrapping his prize.

'Take your jeans off now,' Amelia pleaded, struggling with his flies as he pulled the zip of her catsuit down almost as far as her pubic hair. With his body momentarily apart from hers, the cold breeze of the fan raised goosebumps all across her belly. 'Please.'

'No.' He shook his beautiful head so that the tawny curls of his hair swayed like the leaves of a tree.

'Who's in charge here?' Amelia asked.

'I am,' said Guido.

Amelia closed her green eyes against his most masterful smile as his hand slipped beneath the silky jersey again and brushed oh-so-close to her clitoris. But not quite close enough.

'Oh, yes. Touch me there,' she murmured, trying to decrease the distance between them by pressing her pelvis upwards against his hand. As she moved, her thighs touched and she could feel the wetness creeping down her legs. She felt damp all over now. Glowing.

Guido's finger rubbed tantalisingly against the swollen knot of pleasure that had been longing for his attention. He was breathing noisily, his face in her neck. Amelia twisted her face away from his kiss, her hand stuffed in her mouth to stifle her moans as Guido began to rub harder at the tortured flesh.

'Faster,' she whispered through clenched teeth. But Guido had already decided to move on to something else. He slipped one arm around her waist and lifted her like a rag doll before he carefully eased the catsuit down past her hips so that she was completely exposed at last.

'I was wondering if it was your real colour,' he quipped as he saw in full for the first time the silky red curls of her pubic hair. Amelia was too dizzy with pleasure to take it as an insult. Once more she reached out for the buttons of Guido's fly. Now, at last, he must be ready. The outline of his erection clearly strained against the worn blue cloth of his jeans. And at last he knelt astride her and didn't protest as she worked each silver button free, her eyes full of determination. When the buttons were all undone, Guido stood up from the couch to let the jeans fall from his narrow hips to his feet.

'Hey, you match too,' Amelia laughed.

It was true. Guido's prick stood out proudly from a crop of curls that exactly matched his tawny hair. Amelia lay back with her arms beneath her head and surveyed the full effect as Guido stepped out of his trousers and posed before her, completely naked. No wonder he was a model. He was absolutely perfect from his eyebrows to his toenails. His well-muscled thighs just cried out to be bitten all the way up from his knees to his quivering balls.

Guido moved closer and Amelia reached out a hand to trace a path up the inside of his leg to the tidy sac of his scrotum. As she drew her long painted thumbnail up the inside of his thigh, Guido gasped. The sensation, which was nothing if not supremely pleasurable, caused his prick to jolt upwards with a shudder. Amelia continued to follow the path right along the shivering prick to its end. Then she wrapped her hand fully around it and pulled the foreskin slowly back and forth a couple of times as though she was trying it out for size.

It was big.

Good.

Guido locked his hands behind his head as though he was stretching in the morning sun and just let her play idly with the thick warm shaft for a while. He was obviously used to the adoration. Subconsciously, Amelia let her free hand drop between her own legs, gently feeling the warm, wet haven of her vagina that was missing Guido's attention almost too much to allow her to concentrate on his pleasure at all.

'Oh,' he gasped as his prick jolted upwards in Amelia's hand. Sensing that he might be about to come way too soon, he unwrapped her reluctant fingers and shuddered away the first early spasm.

'Oh yes,' Amelia sighed as Guido dropped spontaneously to his knees beside the couch. She positioned herself so that she had a leg over each of his shoulders. She had slipped the catsuit off altogether now and Guido's succulent mouth was level with her naked, swelling clit.

'Kiss me there,' she murmured.

Guido flicked out his tongue. Now he was teasing her clitoris exactly as he had teased her breasts. Amelia crossed her arms over her chest and hugged herself tightly as she felt a spasm of pleasure rocket through her body when his tongue touched the tiny bundle of nerves for the first time. Guido waited just long enough for the moment to pass before he touched her again and an identical shiver took the place of the one that had died away.

Amelia didn't know what to do with herself. On an impulse, she took hold of the back of his head and pulled him towards her. Laughing, Guido straightened out his long tongue, stiff as any of the pricks Amelia had had the misfortune to meet, and began to use it like a penis to probe inside her, abandoning her clitoris for the narrow, moist passage beneath, parting her labia with his fingers as though they were the petals of some delicate, precious flower.

Amelia didn't let go of his head. Instead she used it to help guide his tongue. In and out. In and out. She felt the moistness of her vagina mingled with his saliva begin to trickle towards her anus. She was so wet. So wet and so ready.

'Fuck me.' She leaned over him and whispered hotly in his ear. 'Fuck me, please.'

Guido had his own hand on his penis now and was pulling it slowly, echoing the thrusts he made into Amelia with his tongue. But it was getting just too hot to carry on like this. Just too hot to play around.

Amelia twisted her fingers in Guido's hair and pulled him up and away from her clitoris until he was level with her face again.

Her eyes flashed.

'I want you to fuck me,' she told him once more.

Guido wiped his mouth with the back of his hand and shook his head.

'Are you refusing to fuck me?' Amelia asked.

Guido took a swig of his half-forgotten drink and nodded.

Amelia slumped back onto the chaise-longue in a huff. But soon Guido was on top of her again and laughing. He wasn't about to leave her aching and unfulfilled. His tongue, cold and wet now from the drink, traced a path from her throat to her ear, sending shivers all over her body. Then he traced the outline of her pouting lips, flickering teasingly between them, denying her penetration anywhere. Just yet.

Amelia made a grab for Guido's penis. It was so

hard. How could he still be holding back? She eased the foreskin up and down as she positioned herself beneath him, raising her pelvis up from the cushions so that the very head of his penis almost kissed her cunt. Guido gasped involuntarily and tried to pull away. Amelia closed her eyes, sure that he must penetrate her now . . . but then, to her amazement, he rolled off her and onto the floor, where he lay spread-eagled on the Chinese rug, his dick pointing straight up to the sky.

'Guido!' Amelia squealed as she leapt down on top of him. She straddled his legs and took his penis in her hands once more, kissing him madly all over his face to distract his attention as she brought herself down onto the stiff, swollen rod.

'Aaaagh, yes.' Guido's eyes were screwed up against the incredible sensation.

'Yes,' Amelia sighed triumphantly. She lowered herself down the silken shaft until her bottom touched the top of Guido's thighs. 'I've got ya. That feels so good,' she murmured through lips dark red with arousal. 'So good.' She eased herself up again, savouring the sensation of his penis passing slowly through her aching labia. The exquisite feeling was making her body sing inside like a bow being drawn across the tight strings of a violin.

'Now doesn't that feel better?' she asked him.

Guido nodded. He had taken her by the hips and was helping her to move. Up and down. Up and down. Slowly at first, but soon gathering speed. He felt so hard. So perfectly, perfectly hard.

Amelia leaned forward and supported herself with her hands on either side of Guido's head. Now the control rested with neither of them. Amelia sighed in ecstasy each time her buttocks brushed Guido's balls. He pushed upwards simultaneously, driving his penis into her, filling her so completely with his long, strong cock. Her body was racked with a delicious quaking, every centimetre of her skin vibrating with joy. Then she leaned backwards until her soft red hair brushed Guido's legs, holding the position for a delicious moment or two until she felt the ability to hold back any longer slip quickly and inexorably away.

Guido's eyes were screwed tightly shut. Fresh sweat gathered on his forehead, which was creased into lines with his effort. Amelia pulled herself upright again and grasped him by the shoulders, unconsciously digging her fingernails into his flesh as she rode him faster and faster and they hurtled towards the climax.

'No, no, no,' Guido cried, while at the same time he was unable to stop himself from grasping Amelia's waist to move her faster and faster up and down his prick. His shaft was beginning to twitch urgently inside her. Her pussy echoed him by tightening its caress. Amelia threw herself forward on top of Guido, her hair covering his face as he pushed upwards and into her body one last desperate time.

They came together. Their bodies were so close that it was as if they had melted into each other. Amelia could barely breathe as her orgasm shook her body, sending a shudder from the back of her neck right down through her quivering thighs. Guido roared as his come left his body, pumping into her, filling her with his desire.

When it was over, Amelia still held him tightly. Her thighs gripped powerfully against his in a full body embrace. Her arms wrapped tightly around his perspiring neck.

They lay like that on the soft Chinese rug until their breathing had synchronised and was steady again.

Chapter Three

AMELIA SIGHED HEAVILY and leaned her sweating forehead against the cool glass of the window. Down below, New York was still very much awake, though it was the middle of the night and the park was in total darkness now, a real no-man's land. Still too hot, Amelia leaned her whole body against the glass, with her arms and legs spread-eagled so that her fingers and toes were almost in the corners of the huge window. She wondered if anyone was looking up. If perhaps someone on the other side of the park had a pair of binoculars trained on her right now. The paparazzi went to some incredible extremes these days to get a picture that the tabloids would pay big bucks for. And what a great picture this would be, Amelia thought idly. Her famous and naked body, full frontal, spread out. There was nothing between her naked curves and New York but an inch or so of see-through glass.

She looked down momentarily at the yellow

taxis which were still spinning by, even at this late hour, twenty-four storeys below. Her heart lurched from her stomach to her mouth and back. What a sensation. She tried to repeat it by looking straight down again, but the fear had already gone. That was the problem with thrills. You always got used to them . . . And how very soon.

In the room behind her she heard the sound of Guido's footsteps as he emerged from the shower and walked towards her, still towel-drying his wavy hair as he crossed the floor. Amelia didn't turn to see him, but watched him approach in reflection. Just before he reached her, he took the towel he was using to dry his hair and wrapped it coyly around his waist.

'The view's really wonderful from up here,' she told him, without turning round. 'You should come and take a look.' She felt Guido's hand rest lightly on the side of her waist as he stepped up behind her on the wide window-seat. He rested his chin lightly on her naked shoulder, not knowing that his stubble scratched her delicate skin.

'You're right,' he said. 'And I should think that the view is really good from over there as well.' He pointed towards the apartments on the other side of the park.

'Do you think there's someone watching us?' Amelia asked mischievously.

'Maybe,' said Guido.

'They'd be getting pretty bored by now.'

'Perhaps they would.'

Guido slid his warm strong hand between

Amelia's hot thighs and casually stroked her clitoris with his index finger as if he was tickling beneath the chin of a cat. Amelia pressed herself harder against the chilly glass, flattening out her breasts. Her clitoris still ached from their encounter on the Chinese rug.

'That feels nice,' she sighed.

'This,' asked Guido as he stroked her clitoris a little harder. 'Or leaning against the window?'

'Both.'

Guido let the towel that he had wrapped around his waist fall to the floor and pushed his now fully naked body closer to Amelia's. She could feel his hard-on, resting firm and warm against the small of her back. She reached behind her and pushed it down a little, at the same time raising herself up on tiptoe so that the welcome shaft sprang between her legs and pressed upwards against her swollen labia. Slowly she eased herself backwards and forwards along its length, lubricating it with the juices that even now were seeping from her longing vagina.

'You're all hard again,' she observed casually.

Guido thrust himself forward between her legs in reply, planting a kiss on her shoulder at the same time. Amelia giggled at the strange sight of his penis head poking out from the red bush of her own pubic hair.

'It looks like it's mine,' she said.

'It is,' Guido whispered. Then he brought his hand around the front of her body and slowly inserted his middle finger into her wet vagina.

'But you are not ready yet, no?' he teased.

Amelia ground her clitoris down against his

27

hand with a groan of disagreement. Then she moved his hand out of the way and took hold of his penis, firmly. She tipped her bottom up towards him and tried to ease the rock-hard shaft into her pussy from behind.

'I might come round to the idea if you get things going for me,' she told him in a whisper.

'Oh, really?'

Parting her labia carefully, Guido slowly inched himself further inside. Amelia breathed in sharply. Their frantic fuck on the floor had left her just a little fragile. Sensing her delicacy, Guido placed his hands flat against the glass and began to thrust slowly and carefully. Amelia twisted her fingers into his and leaned her face against the window again. As she breathed in and out through her open mouth, the glass frosted up, obscuring the beautiful view, a veil of passion.

Carefully, Guido pulled himself from her for just long enough to help her down from the window. Standing on the polished wooden floor now, Amelia placed her hands on the painted sill and leaned forward, waiting for Guido to enter her again. In this position, with her bending over, he had a little more room to manoeuvre and could thrust far deeper than before. Amelia gasped as she felt his balls swing hard against her with each thrust and touch her swelling clitoris.

As he moved lazily in and out of Amelia's longing vagina, Guido ran his hands over the smooth, soft skin of her back. She felt him linger with his fingers in one particular spot and knew that he had found her tiny birthmark. Then she felt a flood of warmth as he leaned forward awkwardly to kiss the spot, covering her back with his body, his fluffy chest hair tickling her as he did so.

'Harder,' she murmured.

As Guido straightened up and increased the tempo to satisfy her, Amelia brought her own hand between her legs. Now, when his balls came forward between her thighs, she stretched her fingers out to touch the warm, fleshy sac. Guido murmured something softly in Italian as she barely brushed his scrotum, her fingertips increasing his pleasure in the way that the ghostly touch of a feather increases the sensitivity of a blushing cheek.

'Ohh! Harder,' Amelia moaned as she began to feel the crescendo of her arousal gathering near. She reached out to steady herself by placing the hand that had been between her legs on the glass. The heat of her palm left an imprint that she would see the next day. Far below them, the impatient taxi drivers of New York still sounded their horns. But Amelia felt as though she needed all the time in the world with this man.

'Is that hard enough?' Guido asked as he pounded into her, simultaneously using her hips to pull her backwards against him so that their bodies crashed together. Amelia nodded but she couldn't find the breath to tell him in words how good she felt at that moment in time. Better than she had felt in an age . . .

The hand on the window which was holding her in position clenched into a fist. The hand between her legs groped frantically for Guido's balls, then her clitoris, massaging it wildly as

Guido pushed deeper and deeper and deeper in.

'Guido,' Amelia panted. 'Guido, Guido, Guido.'

The sound of her voice calling out his name was too much for him. Guido couldn't contain himself any longer. He felt his prick spasm into ultimate hardness inside her soft body. His taut thighs tensed into position against the curve of her rounded buttocks. His fingers tightened around the narrow contours of her tiny waist.

'Amelia!' he cried to the ceiling as the first jets of come burst forth from a penis which felt like a burning rod of steel. Amelia threw her head back and cried out with him as her vagina began to contract around him, pumping the come from his body with spasms too powerful to control. She shuddered with the force of her orgasm and grasped to hold onto the body behind her. Her legs began to tremble as she was racked with pleasure again. Guido pounded on, not stopping or even slowing down until Amelia could feel the cocktail of their mingled juices begin to creep down her thigh.

Chapter Four

'*ONE MORE TIME,*' said Guido.

Amelia grinned at him through her untidy hair. This Italian certainly had staying-power. 'OK,' Amelia said. 'But this time, I'm in charge.' Guido nodded eagerly. 'And I'm on top,' she added. He didn't complain, thinking that it would be nice to lie down for a bit. Amelia rose from the chaise-longue, upon which she had been curled up like a cat for the past giddy hour, and took him by the hand to lead him into the bedroom. It was the one part of her elegant suite they had yet to discover that night.

Inside the bedroom the huge bed was covered in so many cuddly toys that you could barely see the sheets beneath. The toys were gifts from Amelia's fans that Rowena insisted on arranging in cohorts along the pillows whenever they arrived at a new hotel. But now Amelia brushed them brutally aside, sending bears and rabbits and fluffy green frogs flying off the bed, smacking into the fitted wardrobes. There was only one toy she wanted beneath her covers that evening.

'Make yourself comfortable, Guido,' she told him. 'Oh, and I suppose I ought to say "Any last requests" as well.'

'I don't think so,' said Guido with a naive smile. He stretched himself out in the very middle of the bed with his arms crossed beneath his head and his feet crossed at the ankle. Amelia was fiddling about in her wardrobe. When she turned back to the prone Adonis she tutted loudly and said, 'No, that really won't do.'

Guido shrugged. He didn't understand. She'd said 'make yourself comfortable' and he had.

Amelia explained.

'You really need to spread your legs . . . baby.'

Guido nodded and obeyed unquestioningly. He even continued to grin as Amelia fastened first his wrists and then his ankles to the corners of the Elizabethan-style four-poster bed. She had lots of rope in her wardrobe, she explained, because she had been using it in one of her videos. Not a video that would be likely to be seen on MTV, of course, but Guido didn't ask about that.

Guido strained against his bonds. 'Too loose,' he laughed as his right hand easily popped free. Amelia tied the knot again and gritted her teeth as she pulled it as tight as she could with her foot pressed against the side of the bed for leverage as she tugged.

'Too loose now?' she asked, panting from the exertion.

'Er . . . no.' Guido looked at his hand, which had been going red but was now looking distinctly white as the blood drained away. 'No,' he reassured her, twisting his wrist to ensure that he wasn't about to lose circulation in all his extremities. 'That will be just fine.'

'Good.'

Amelia stood at the end of the bed for a moment or two just admiring her handiwork. Guido pulled faces at her, pouting, playing.

'Oh dear, what are you going to do to me now?' he said in a voice of mock horror.

'I'm going to have my wicked way with you,' said Amelia, as she let the jade wrap drop from her shoulders onto the floor and climbed onto the bed so that she was kneeling between his legs.

She moved forward on all fours until her face was just above his dick. She lowered her lips to the shaft – it was only semi-hard – and licked a trail from his furry balls to the very tip of its head. It twitched into life immediately.

'Thank goodness for that,' Amelia smiled. She followed the path that her tongue had taken with a long red fingernail. Guido screwed up his eyes.

'Carefully,' he warned her.

'Be quiet or I'll have to gag you,' she replied, dipping her head to take his penis into her mouth once more. Guido moaned as she let her tongue touch just the eye of the smooth dome which already glistened with a drop of semen. Just the tip of her tongue reached out again and again to him, tantalising the delicate ridge of his raphe as her hands roamed carelessly over his balls. Then she sucked him fully in, enclosing him in her mouth and pumping him with her tongue. He muttered something in Italian that she took to be a good sign.

When she was satisfied that he was finally hard enough, Amelia rose from her position on all fours and straddled her prisoner. Guido bit his lips as she hovered above his dick but first she playfully placed her own finger in her crotch. 'Ready?' she asked. Guido's cock twitched as if in reply, then stood to attention, like a mast without a flag. Slowly, tantalisingly, draining every bit of pleasure she could from the anticipation, Amelia began to lower herself down towards him without taking her eyes from his.

At first, she took only the tip inside her and waited for barely a second before she began slowly to ease herself up again. Guido shuddered at the sensation, his mouth unable to contain a sigh. The next time, Amelia went just a little deeper, her thighs quivering with the tremendous effort of resisting the urge to plunge him into her, right up to the hilt. Guido's hands tensed into fists, longing to reach out and grab her and force her body down. His eyes were closed in delirious pleasure.

By the time she made her third journey down, it had almost become too much. Amelia groaned in ecstasy as her bottom brushed Guido's balls and he pushed upwards as far as he could at the same time, driving himself into her, impaling her, filling her with his gorgeous cock. Amelia's body was racked with a delicious quaking, every nerve-ending was singing with joy. She arched her body backwards and held that position for as long as she could, relishing the feeling of completeness before she carried on.

Guido's eyes were still closed. Beads of sweat began to gather on his forehead as Amelia rocked on his prick. Determined to heighten the sensation still further, she reached behind her and teased his scrotal sac with a careful stroke from her long red fingernails. Guido moaned urgently. His shaft reacted to the teasing touch by twitching inside her. Her pussy tightened against it in response.

'You feel sooo good!' he told her, still longing to grasp hold of her waist with both hands to help her move up and down ever faster. Instead he could do nothing but thrash from side to side in his bonds, desperate to break even one hand free. Amelia grasped handfuls of her own hair as the pleasure began to reach a dangerous intensity. Her vagina grasped for Guido's penis.

'I'm going to come! I'm going to come,' Guido groaned as his hips drove him further into her one more time. It was too late to slow down now. Amelia's pussy contracted again and again, and her orgasm burst from her like a peal of laughter.

'Yes, yes, yeess!'

Amelia felt herself bounced upwards by Guido's bucking hips. She punched the air as she came down again, feeling a powerful surge wrack her body like a bolt of electricity straight from the mains. 'Yes! Yes! Yes!' Guido panted like a pig. His thighs shuddered with exertion. His face was almost surprised. 'Yes! No! Yes!'

His come exploded from him like a French missile in the Pacific.

Amelia was thrown forward on top of him by the power of his final thrust. Straightaway, she took his face in her hands and kissed him passionately as her own orgasm finally overwhelmed her, sending waves of pleasure shuddering along her vaginal walls.

They lay still. Inside their bodies, the waves subsided. The spasms were growing further and further apart. Amelia lay on top of Guido with his penis still inside her until she felt it grow soft and begin to slip away. His breathing had changed. It was softer. Slower. She guessed that he must almost be asleep.

Amelia kissed him tenderly on the neck and finally tore herself away from him with just a little regret. She went to take a shower. When she came back into the bedroom, she looked fondly at the man still lying in the same position on her bed. His face in sleep had lost some of its years. His mouth was curled upwards in a goofy kind of smile.

Amelia checked that the ropes which tied his hands and feet to the bed-posts weren't too tight, then she took a blanket from the cupboard and installed herself on the biggest sofa in the sitting-room.

She fell asleep watching the sun come up over Central Park.

Chapter Five

'I WANT TO take some time off, that's all.'

It was not the best news that Rowena had heard that day.

'You what?'

'I said, I want to take some time off.'

'But you went to St Barts.'

'Yes, last November! Look, Rowena, I've been on tour for almost a whole year now. It's getting ridiculous. I haven't seen my family. I haven't seen any of my friends. I haven't even seen my cat.'

'Your cat is in the best boarding-house money could buy.'

'Yeah, and I bet she finds that a real consolation. Look, I know that you've been really good to me, Rowena. And I know that I wouldn't be where I am today if it wasn't for your faith in me and your determination that I could make it . . . But now I have made it, and quite frankly, I'm sick of it. I don't have a life any more. I feel like I'm under observation every minute of the day –

especially since Frankenstein's been on the job.'

Rowena and Amelia both sneaked a look to see if the six foot eight lump of muscle had heard his name being taken in vain. Franklin sat on a hard chair in the corner of Rowena's makeshift hotel room office nodding his ponderous head. He was wearing his Walkman and almost certainly listening to Whitesnake.

'I think he could use a break as well,' Amelia ventured, in attempt to make her request for time off seem almost altruistic. 'I could certainly use a break from him.'

'But you haven't finished the tour,' said Rowena firmly. 'You have twenty-three sold out dates from here to Los Angeles. And the money has already changed hands.'

'Tell them that I'm ill or something,' Amelia pleaded. 'You could tell them that I've hurt my throat.'

'I won't do that,' Rowena replied flatly. 'Though if you push me very much more I may well end up hurting your throat myself.'

Amelia gazed out of the window. From Rowena's room she could see the Empire State Building and thought jealously of the tourists looking down on the city from that skyscraper right now. The people who were on holiday in New York. Taking time out. Before it actually happened, Amelia had been under the impression that being a rock star would give her the opportunity to do exactly what she wanted, whenever she wanted. How wrong had she been? She had far less freedom now.

Rowena had already launched into her 'You're

not just a person, you're an industry,' speech. How many people would she be letting down? Hundreds. Thousands. Hundreds of thousands, if she included the adoring fans.

'OK. I think I've heard this one before,' Amelia cut Rowena short. 'Listen, how long do I have before the next show?'

'We're in Cleveland next Tuesday. You see, you have a whole free week,' Rowena said brightly.

'So I could do my own thing until Monday?'

'Well,' Rowena chewed her lip and flipped through the pages of her chunky diary. 'Not exactly, sweetheart. You have rehearsals from nine to five, Tuesday through Sunday.'

'Eight hours of rehearsal a day?' Amelia shrieked. 'That's ridiculous.'

'We've got some big shows coming up. They'll be on TV. The dancers need the practice and it does company morale good for you to be there too.'

'Company morale? What am I? A PLC?'

Rowena frowned like a headmistress tolerating the ramblings of a fifth-form truant.

'OK. OK. Who needs a holiday? I'll just go and get a facial instead.' Amelia shrugged her shoulders and got ready to go back to her own room.

'Good girl,' Rowena smiled, convinced by Amelia's capitulation. She put a tick against something in her diary and began to look for a number on her Psion.

Amelia hesitated at the door. 'I think I'll have a bath first.'

There's no better place to think than in the bath, Amelia decided after leaving Rowena alone with her small triumph. The hotel's most luxurious penthouse suite had two huge bathrooms, one for each of the enormous bedrooms. The bathrooms were pretty much identical except in colour. One had a champagne-coloured suite which was complemented by a candelabrum and fluffy gold trimmed towels, while the other was decked out in Caribbean blue. That day Amelia chose the blue suite, since it suited her contemplative mood.

As she took off the faded jeans and the T-shirt that she had stolen from Guido that morning, Amelia wondered what he had put on to go home. She couldn't find the Chinese silk dressing-gown that she had discarded and her mind conjured up a sudden image of Guido rushing through the hotel lobby to catch a cab in the riotous jade green wrap. Oh, Guido had been worth his weight in gold. And if that morning's incident hadn't boosted his chances of a career in the lime-light then nothing would. Still, perhaps she should try and track him down, Amelia thought. Send him a present to say 'sorry for the inconvenience' or something like that. She waggled her finger through a hole in the seat of his stolen pants. A new pair of jeans perhaps?

Amelia turned the stiff marble taps until the water finally began to cascade into the bath and fill the mirror-tiled room with steam. She watched as her reflection disappeared in the mirror over the shallow sink. With one finger she traced the outline of her face and its features in the condensation. Though over the straight glum line of her unhappy lips she drew a smiley mouth.

She should be so happy, she told herself for the third or fourth time that day. Thousands of people would be happy to give up their freedom for a life of constant hot water in bathrooms as luxurious as this. It certainly beat washing in the Ganges . . .

The water swirled halfway up the sides of the bath now. Amelia took a bottle of bubble bath from the freshly stocked shelf and poured two generous capfuls into the whirlpool beneath the taps. Quickly the floral-scented bubbles began to form and spread out to cover the whole surface with an inch-deep layer of foam. Amelia trailed her fingers in the water to see whether it was warm enough yet. Not too hot. Just perfect. She screwed the taps shut and began to climb in, big toe first.

She stood in the water which came halfway up her calves and sighed as she folded her body up until she was sitting down with the foam around her shoulders. She piled her hair up high on top of her head and secured it there Japanese-style with a pair of wooden pins, each one topped off with a curly white shell. She had dragged the stereo from her bedroom as near to the bathroom door as the cable would allow and now it was playing out a cello suite by Bach. Something she couldn't sing along with. She needed to rest her throat.

Slowly Amelia slid down in the water until the

bubbles tickled her chin. Then she lay back and savoured the sensation of a thousand tiny prickles as the bubbles began to burst against her skin.

For a few minutes she simply lay there, completely still, luxuriating in the warmth of the scented water around her and the rich, deep sound of the cello. In her mind, she wasn't in New York any more, but in a place where work and fame didn't matter. Lazily she reached for the washcloth which rested on the side of the bath and began to stroke her body clean of worry with long, sweeping movements that left her skin tingling in their path.

Amelia shifted so that one of her knees poked up out of the bubbles like an iceberg emerging from the waves. She noted, not for the first time, how very pale her skin was, even when it was flushed with the heat of the bath. Amelia scrubbed at her knee lazily. At least her job allowed her enough visits to the beauty clinic to ensure that even her rough bits were smooth, she thought to herself with a sad half-smile.

And the tour would be over soon, she reasoned. Just another month and then Rowena couldn't possibly refuse to let her have a proper holiday. But Amelia knew that even when the tour had finished, the circus wouldn't. The record company execs were already baying for something new. A new song, a new single, a new album to be released in time for next Christmas. Amelia was suddenly aware that she hadn't written a new song in months – instead she had just played the old tunes over and over again. She wasn't even sure that she could write anything new any more.

Nothing made her feel like writing these days.

The bath had one silvered button, the size of a ten pence piece, set in its side. It was the button for the jetstream. Sighing, Amelia sought it out beneath the cover of the bubbles, walking her fingers along the smooth side of the bath until she found it. She gave the button a determined little press and the jets sprang into action. Immediately the sound of the cello was all but drowned out by the noisy churning of the pump. The burst bubbles were rejuvenated by its action and pretty soon they were floating as high as Amelia's nose. She playfully snorted some out of her face, sending them drifting like feathers to the floor. The powerful jets pummelled her thighs until they almost ached.

'I'm forever blowing bubbles!' she sang. Perhaps she could release a cover version of that.

After a while Amelia grew tired of sitting in the same position. She rolled onto her side and tried to make a pillow of the back of the bath. It wasn't comfortable. It was as hard against her ear as it had been on the back of her neck but, just as she was about to give up the idea of actually getting comfortable, she found a position which was very much worth holding.

As she lay, half on her side, the jet which had been playing against her right thigh was now playing right between her legs. She let out a small gasp of pleasure as the realisation first hit her that if she shifted only a little more, the jet would be right against her clitoris. The effect was instant.

Amelia felt a blossoming of her clitoris with a speed and intensity she had never experienced before. She gripped the side of the bath to keep herself in the same spot as her body tried to jerk away from the intense sensation. She forced her body back as it tried to arch forward. She lowered her bottom towards the source of the water so that the power of the jet was stronger still.

'Oh, my ... I ... I ... ' Amelia gasped in surprise. She sat quickly upright and let the feeling subside. She was blushing, almost embarrassed by her peculiar discovery. Moments later the jets stopped automatically. Amelia added a little more hot water to the bath. She rubbed thoughtfully at the back of her neck with a washcloth.

The Bach cello suite had hit a quiet patch.

Amelia passed the washcloth over her hot face. She looked down at her breasts. Despite the heat in the bathroom, her nipples stood out as if caught in an icy blast. She felt so horny, it was ridiculous. Surreptitiously, as if someone else might be watching, Amelia reached down beneath the thinning bubbles and pressed the jetstream button once more.

The bubbles burst into action.

Amelia clung to the slippery side of the bath with one white-knuckled hand while below the water her other hand, as if it didn't belong to the same body, crept down to where the powerful stream was pummelling her into an orgasm. Her hips bucked already, though she knew she wasn't quite there. But this was better than any vibrator she had ever tried. Amelia's fingers touched her swollen clitoris carefully, drawing back almost instantly at first because the power was almost too great. But pretty soon she felt that she was reaching a plateau. The jet, though effective, was just not human enough. Her body longed for a touch that it recognised to finish the whole act off.

Carefully Amelia parted the lips of her vagina and moved slightly forward so that the jet no longer played on her clitoris but instead was shooting right into her, an aqua-dildo that made her writhe with joy. Then she rolled slowly over onto her other side, allowing her body a few moments to recover. This time she knew the position she was looking for and found it right away. She gasped as the jet played against her, massaging her into ecstasy. She parted her labia with her fingers again and moaned with desire as she slipped two fingers inside.

The spasms started suddenly, spreading quickly throughout her body. She felt the muscles contract against her own fingers, as if her body was trying to pull them further in. 'Ohmigod, yes!' Amelia squealed, sending a wave of water out over the side of the bath and onto the floor as she jolted upright and quivered with an orgasm that felt like laughter running through her veins.

Finally, when the jetstream had finished again and turned itself off, Amelia sank beneath the bubbles until the water closed warm over her smiling face. She lay there for as long as she could hold her breath, enjoying the sense of total calm which came from having had a fantastic orgasm with a partner that had the added advantage of turning back into a perfectly well-mannered warm bath afterwards. At last she floated back up to the surface and took a deep long breath to the bottom of her lungs.

'Whoah,' she sighed. She felt so relaxed. And her mind was so completely clear.

Singing as she did so, Amelia rinsed the suds out of her hair. Then she worked the plug out of its socket with her toes and leapt out of the bath into the faithful arms of a fluffy white towel.

Chapter Six

SO, ONE BATH later, Amelia had made a decision. Sod the world tour. Sod the fans. She needed a rest and she was going home to London to see her friends and her cat if it was the very last thing she did.

And less than eight hours after leaving Rowena's office in such a state of sorry submission, she was boarding Concorde back to London. By the time Rowena discovered that Amelia had gone, it would be too late – she would be halfway across the Atlantic. Maybe she would even be pushing a trolley full of luggage and duty-free cigarettes through the arrivals lounge at Heathrow. Amelia laughed as she crept out through the staff entrance to the hotel and climbed into a waiting taxi. She couldn't think why she hadn't done it before.

'It's time to escape!' she sang as she tried to hurry through passport control. That was a mistake, since it was one of her own songs and she found herself having to sign half a dozen autographs before the customs officers would let her go. Still, once she had done that, they were decent enough not to insist on searching through her knickers.

When she finally boarded the plane, Amelia found herself sitting next to a rather elegant-looking man. He introduced himself briefly before take-off. His name was Crispin Hardcastle and he was in finance. Amelia introduced herself as a musician and he didn't ask for details, so she offered him none. When the plane was safely in the air and the hostesses had brought round the second glass of complimentary champagne, Crispin reclined his seat as far as it would go and closed his eyes.

Amelia glanced up from her magazine and took a better look at her neighbour. He really was very handsome. His narrow nose was perfectly straight. His lashes just long enough to brush his cheeks. His hair, which swept gracefully back from his forehead, had obviously been very black once, but was now flecked with grey. Amelia guessed him to be in his forties, though his waist showed no hint of middle-age spread. She made a decision that by the time she left the plane she would have his phone number.

As the plane cruised at twenty thousand feet, Amelia leaned her head against the window and looked out at the world which passed below. Greenland sped by without the faintest hint of green. Iceland likewise, before the plane began to turn right over Scotland and head for home. Amelia wondered what Rowena would be saying, or rather screaming, now. Whether she would have thought that Amelia would go to such lengths for a little bit of peace and quiet. She remembered in a patchwork dozens of flights with Rowena and the band. Always jet-lagged. Always crippled with leg cramps no matter how sumptuous the first-class seat. Then she remembered a flight before the touring started. Before her career started. Flying back from Las Vegas after her mother's fifth wedding. That was the one where she married the dentist, who had been replaced by a landscape gardener now. Amelia remembered how Karis had turned up to surprise her at her hotel.. How the weekend had suddenly become much more eventful.

Amelia almost laughed out loud at the memory of one particular cowboy in his underpants.

Karis. They had seen even less of each other over the last year though Karis had finally moved from Los Angeles to London, to set up home with the record producer who had once been Amelia's man. That hadn't lasted, of course. But now it seemed that Karis had found the man of her dreams. A rugby international, apparently. And to think that Karis had never even heard of the game before Tim came into her life. However, within weeks of that fateful meeting in the Dean Street Piano and Pitcher bar, Karis had dumped her trademark ruby red shoes for a pair of wellies and was spending her Saturdays shivering on the muddy edges of windblown fields. Amelia made a note to look Karis out as soon as she landed. In fact, she might go and stay with Karis instead of at her own place, to put Rowena off the scent for just a little longer.

While Amelia considered the various possibilities open to her when she got back home, her recent late nights crept up on her and she drifted off to sleep. She didn't wake up until the plane had touched down and Crispin Hardcastle had gone. Without giving her his number.

In the event, Amelia went back to her own place first. The flat smelled horribly stale. No one had been in there since the tour started way back in March. On the windowsill of the kitchen even the hardiest of Amelia's cacti were gasping a final spiky breath. A huge pile of letters had made it difficult to open the front door. Amelia flicked through the dusty envelopes as she wandered around the silent rooms to survey the damage of six months of neglect.

Bills, bills, junk mail, bills. There was only one letter that looked as though it might be worth reading. Amelia slit open the pink envelope with a kitchen knife as she waited for the kettle to boil so that she could make a decent cup of tea. She congratulated herself on having had the foresight to sneak a couple of one portion milk cartons off the hostess trolley on the plane.

'Dearest Amy,' the letter began. 'Have been trying to call you for weeks but you're never in one place for long enough and your security staff are harder to get through than the jerks on the gate at the White House. It's been ages since I've seen you, though I've been charting your progress on 'Top of the Pops'. Was that Whitney Houston cover you did really such a good idea? All is fine here. I even visited your cat at the cattery the other week. She misses you, as you might expect. But, hey, let me get to the point of this letter, since you know from school that writing was never my strong point. The thing is, Amelia, that while you've been away, Tim and I have been getting closer and closer. Neither of us is all that young any more and so, you're never going to believe this, Amy, but we've decided to do it. We've decided to tie the knot . . .'

Amelia's jaw fell to her chest.

'Tie the knot! Karis!'

Amelia tipped the pink envelope upside down, shaking frantically, and, sure enough, a crisp white invitation card printed with extravagant silver writing floated to the ground.

'The wedding of Karis Eugenia Lusardi to Tim Williamson . . . 4th September . . . St James's Church . . .'

Amelia laughed in disbelief. Karis was getting married? Karis 'Loose Elastic' Lusardi was beating her to the altar. And in just another four days time. Incredible! Within seconds, Amelia was dialling the unfamiliar phone number at the top of Karis's alarming letter. Thank goodness Amelia had chosen to come home when she did. This particular wedding she quite simply had to see.

'I know it probably seems a little strange,' Karis began, 'but you know, Amelia, it is possible for people to change and I've decided that all along, all through that terrible period when we would sleep with anything we could pin down for long enough, I wasn't really in it for the sex . . . I was simply looking for love . . . And now, with Tim, I've found it.'

Amelia could feel her eyes glazing over as it became a bigger and bigger struggle to hold the telephone to her ear.

'Tim is quite simply the most wonderful person I have ever met,' Karis continued. 'He's so steady.'

For steady, read boring, thought Amelia.

'And funny.'

Inane.

'And charming.'

A snob.

'Everybody loves him.'

Everybody loved Mr Blobby.

'But I'm so glad you're back because now I can have a bridesmaid. I wasn't going to bother since I thought that you wouldn't be here.'

'I'd be honoured,' Amelia sighed. 'There will have to be a hen night, of course.'

'A sedate one.'

Amelia replaced the phone as if in a dream. Had that conversation really taken place? Had she been speaking to Karis Lusardi or one of the Stepford wives?

She left the answer-machine on so that it would screen her calls while she recovered from the shock.

As she lay on the sofa, soaking up the top quality British soaps she had missed so much while she was touring, she kept one ear tuned in to the constant stream of rings and blips, just in case someone she actually felt like talking to wanted to speak to her. Rowena had left fifteen messages in half an hour.

'Hi, I'm not here right now. You can reach me

care of Rowena Martin Management.' The cassette was surely almost full.

'If only I could. Amelia Ashton, this is Rowena Martin, calling for the sixteenth time in an hour to offer you your very last chance ever of working in the music business again.'

Rowena was shrieking. This time Amelia just had to give in. Sighing, she forced herself up from the sofa and picked up the phone, cutting off the answer-machine as she did so.

'OK. OK. You can stop shouting now.'

'Amelia! You're there,' Rowena lost her stride. 'What on earth are you doing? We've been worried sick!'

'Yeah, right.'

'Don't be like that.' Amelia was surprised at the sudden softness of Rowena's tone. 'We were worried. We miss you, baby. We care for you, that's all.'

'You just care about your record sales. I'm not coming back until Monday, Rowena. I've just found out that my best friend is getting married on Friday and I have to be at the wedding.'

'But you promise to be back on Monday? OK. That's fine. We'll book you on the Concorde for Sunday afternoon.' Rowena sounded way too calm.

'But you realise that I won't make it back in time for the Cleveland gig?'

'No problem. It's under control.' Amelia knitted her brows together. Had somebody been slipping something in Rowena's tea?

'So you're having a nice relaxing time?' Rowena asked.

Amelia agreed.

'Keeping your diary clear for a couple of days?'

Amelia agreed again.

'Fancy doing your favourite manager a teensy weensy favour?'

'Oh no.' Amelia should have seen it coming. 'Rowena, if you are going to ask me to do anything more stressful than pick something up from Harvey Nichols the answer is a resounding no.'

Rowena dropped the nice girl act immediately. 'A resounding no indeed. Well, madam, I think that under the circumstances you owe us all a big one.'

'I owe you a big one?' Amelia gasped in disbelief. 'You wouldn't have a job without me!'

'Wrong, Amelia,' Rowena countered. 'You are not the biggest fish in my ocean . . .'

'Oh yeah? Last week I was the fastest selling singer on the surface of the earth. Tell me, Rowena, who is top haddock these days.'

'Tracey Gostello,' Rowena said flatly.

'That old crooner?'

'That rich old crooner,' Rowena corrected. 'Rich and influential. Heaven knows you don't deserve it, Amelia, but he actually wants you to sing backing vocals on one of his new tracks. He's recording in London and, praise the lord for small mercies, you have chosen to go back to London instead of some obscure Scottish Isle, and so you are in the right place at the right time to do the job. I've pencilled you in for tomorrow morning. The session will be at Elephant's Eye Studios in Fitzrovia. Shouldn't take you more than half a day.'

'And if I don't want to do it?'

'Darling, there's a saying here on the East Coast that "what goes up must come down". In a very short time you may be glad of the royalties this single will bring you. Particularly if you're going to start throwing tantrums.'

Chapter Seven

IT WAS SETTLED then. That night, before she went to bed, Amelia took the unusual step of setting her alarm clock and by nine in the morning she was sitting in the reception at Elephant's Eye, trying to get a cup of tea out of the apprentice studio engineer who was so amazed to see a real star so early on a Tuesday morning that he kept forgetting what it was that she had asked for.

Tracey Gostello – it was his real name apparently – was late. His entourage cursed him for setting yet another early session that he obviously had little intention of getting up for. As Amelia sipped her tea, complete with two sugars that she hadn't asked for, Gostello's manager fielded phonecalls with increasing irritation. Each one seemed to be from a hysterical girl nursing a badly fractured heart.

'No, Marion, I don't know where he stayed last night. I'm his manager, not his mother. He said he would call you? Then I'm sure there's a perfectly good explanation why he didn't . . . No, I don't know if he's seeing another girl . . . You'll have to check the tabloids.'

As he hung up on the latest groupie, Gostello's manager looked in Amelia's direction and raised his eyebrows in a tired sort of way.

'All these bloody women, and not one of them calling up for me,' he said in his South London wide-boy drawl. 'Like flies round shit, they are. Don't you bloody well go falling for him too, will ya, love?'

'I'll try to resist him,' Amelia replied.

At that moment a hush descended on the busy room. Making his entrance with a lithe yet busty blonde upon his arm, Tracey Gostello tossed his red velvet coat to the apprentice engineer and kissed his astonished manager on the top of his balding head.

'Sorry I'm late, everybody.'

'That's all right, Tracey,' said the manager as he hushed with a stern look a murmur of discontent from the musicians.

Amelia glanced at her watch. He was a whole hour late in fact. She could have used that extra time in bed. The jet-lag was starting to hurt. Badly.

'Let's get to work, shall we?' Gostello marched straight on through to studio four, his entourage following obediently behind him like Moses' tribe strolling across the bottom of the Red Sea. Amelia gathered up her bag and the score she had been reading and shuffled along behind them. Tracey Gostello. What a poser! He hadn't even acknowledged her presence.

57

Once inside the studio, Gostello took the centre chair of three behind the vast and highly complicated mixing desk. His manager sat on one side. The blonde took the other. The engineer, robbed of his place by the girl of the morning, flitted about them nervously, trying to tweak various controls on the desk without getting in the great one's way.

'Quick conference,' Gostello announced, summoning the musicians towards him by waving his hands.

The musicians gathered in front of the desk, already muttering about working conditions and overtime. Amelia joined them. She nodded at a guy she recognised as the drummer from an advertising session she had done a couple of years before. He nodded back and blushed.

'Right,' Gostello began. 'As you know, I don't have much time to do this album. I'm flying back out to the States on Sunday and I want everything to be perfect before I go. That means that I have to demand your full concentration today, ladies and gentlemen, your dedication to the cause. Now, I think everyone's here. Let's have a head count. Martin. Lester . . . Andy . . . good to see you're out of rehab again. Who else? Backing vocals?'

Gostello looked straight at and yet straight through Amelia. Everyone else in the room turned to see who she was.

'You the singer?' Gostello asked.

'Yes,' said Amelia indignantly. 'I'm the singer.' Surely she didn't look that unrecognisable without her make-up on.

'I thought I asked for a name,' Gostello

remarked to his manager in a *faux* whisper. A titter ran through the assembled musicians who knew very well that the only bigger name in the business was Madonna. Amelia felt herself colour red. Gostello smoothed back his hair with an ugly smirk. 'OK. Let's go,' he said, punching the air in a gesture that was intended to be motivational. 'I'll lay down my track first.'

Amelia was fuming. What sweet revenge this must have been for Rowena, landing her in the same room as the biggest jerk in the music industry, if not the biggest jerk in the whole goddamn world. Rumour had it that Tracey Gostello couldn't go on stage without getting one of his backing girls to give him a blow-job first, claiming that it relieved his stress and improved their voices to boot. Well, he had another think coming if he thought that Amelia's contract would extend that far. And fancy him acting as though he didn't know who she was! Even if he had never heard a single note from her repertoire, which was most unlikely, he would at least have seen Amelia's picture plastered all over the walls at Rowena's office.

From the studio's live room, Amelia could hear a strangled wail, followed by a prolonged bout of coughing. They hadn't been able to get a good take yet and Gostello had been in there warbling like a dying cat for almost two whole hours. The blonde he had brought with him was still at the desk, filing her nails with an open bottle of nail varnish sitting precariously close to the mixing desk controls. The engineer looked on in torment as he tried to think of a subtle way to ask the superstar to take it from the top just one more time.

Suddenly the blonde pressed the button that allowed the engineer to talk to the artist through the soundproofing of the live room.

'I'm bored, honey,' she announced in an awful strangled voice. It didn't seem possible that it belonged to someone with such a beautiful face. 'I'm going to go shopping for a bit.'

'OK, darling. See you later.' Gostello waved from his glass chamber, looking more than faintly disgruntled. The blonde teetered out past the guitarists who were sitting on the floor. They made the most of the opportunity to look right up her skirt. Amelia was sure that she enjoyed it. Hmm. Gostello's choice of human accessories did little to raise her opinion of him. At least her own groupie, Guido, had some semblance of charm, wit and intelligence. That blonde was so, so disposable. And by letting herself get 'bored' while watching the work of the master, she had probably signed the death warrant on her passport to fame by proxy already. Suddenly Amelia caught herself having these terrible thoughts and felt horribly ashamed. Why did it matter? Was she jealous of that old tart?

She turned her attention back to the hacking figure in the live room. No, surely she was not. I mean, look at the hairline on that man, she told herself. Gostello could have taken a tip or two from Elton John . . . or Russ Abbot.

At the end of the session, the musicians practically ran for the bar next door to the studio. They hadn't been allowed a proper break all day. Amelia, however, had to stay behind for just a while longer. Rowena had phoned Elephant's Eye to see how her protégée was doing and the call had been put through to the studio. While Amelia chatted, Gostello and his own manager were deep in conversation as they waited for the flustered engineer to label up the DATs which carried the results of a very hard day's work.

'Amelia, isn't it?' Gostello smarmed when she had put down the phone and was gathering up her things in readiness to go back home. 'You sang very well today. I must admit that I was a little reluctant to use you on that track since your sound is so . . . well, so very different from mine. But Rowena insisted and despite my initial doubts, I have to admit that I'm very very pleased with your work.'

'Why thank you,' Amelia replied through tight lips. Praise indeed, she supposed, but still she barely looked at him and carried on buttoning up her jacket.

Gostello shrugged on his ridiculous opera coat and started to head for the door. Then, to her surprise, he turned to look at her again, with a faintly quizzical smile upon his wrinkled nut-brown face. Suddenly he asked, 'I was wondering whether you would care to join me for dinner. I have a reservation for two at Mezzo. Downstairs, of course.'

'What about your girlfriend?' Amelia replied flatly.

'My girlfriend?' Gostello looked confused for a moment before he was hit with a vague recollection of that morning's blonde. 'Oh,

Anastasia?' He tugged at his collar. 'She's not my girlfriend. Just a friend of a friend. I was showing her around the town.'

'How very kind of you.'

'I always try to help my friends when I can,' he smarmed. 'Then you'll join me for dinner?'

Amelia looked down at her tired feet in their too-tight shoes and smiled to herself at the thought of the thousands of women who would have killed to hear that offer. Right now for Amelia however, the thought of a nice hot bath full of Radox had an equally strong pull on her desires. She did a mental calculation. Maybe she should give him the benefit of the doubt. After all, Tracey Gostello had sold twenty million albums. At least he would pick up the tab. And it might even be amusing.

'Mezzo, you say?' Amelia replied brightly. 'Do they do vegetarian?'

In the car to the restaurant, Gostello made a hopelessly indiscreet call on his mobile phone, requesting that his 'guest' be moved to 'more suitable accommodation' before he got back home. Never walk out on a maestro, eh, Amelia thought.

So Anastasia had to pack up her bags while Amelia glided across the polished wooden floor of the entrance lobby at Mezzo on the arm of Tracey Gostello. They were ushered straight downstairs, where they were shown to a table with a blue upholstered seat that looked as though it had been ripped straight out of a Waltzer. The huge curvy banquette which threw them together at its middle was for privacy, Gostello explained. Amelia's lips twisted into a wry smile. The kind of man who chose the biggest restaurant in Europe for privacy was not really the kind of man who minded being recognised once in a while. Even as she was thinking that, a paparazzo leapt out in front of their table and shot off a roll of film. Gostello made a big show of half-hiding his face behind the menu. Amelia smiled widely. After all, the paparazzo probably had a family to feed – and her own reputation was probably shot to pieces anyway after the Guido incident. Amelia did hope that the photographers had managed to get Guido's good side.

'Bloody paparazzi,' Gostello snapped. When the photographer had gone, he reached inside his jacket pocket and pulled out a tiny compact. He studied his reflection from various angles and when he was satisfied that he had nothing stuck between his teeth or some other horror like that, he started to calm down. Amelia pretended not to have noticed.

The food they ordered was fairly *nouvelle*, and Amelia merely picked at the beautiful arrangement of vegetables which were drowned in too much spice. Gostello didn't touch his food at all. Instead he ordered another bottle of Burgundy, going straight for the most expensive bottle on the menu without giving its suitability to Amelia's food a second thought. The wine waiter poured the bottle out mouthful after mouthful, in the way that he had been taught, but pretty soon, Gostello was gulping it at such a rate that the waiter gave up on etiquette and brought out a bigger glass.

Amelia sipped at a mineral water and found herself almost falling out of the seat as she moved to avoid Gostello's wandering hands.

'I've always fancied you,' Gostello murmured hotly in her ear. 'Especially after you did that album, 'Little Earthquakes' or whatever it was called.'

He had mistaken her for Tori Amos. But Amelia didn't like to point it out.

'You've got really great hair, you know.' He placed his bearish paw of a hand on her knee and squeezed it playfully. 'I would really like to have that dangling in my face while you sit on top of me, slowly easing up and down my massive prick.'

Amelia's mouth dropped open. 'I'm sorry?'

'Yeah, I'm hard just thinking about it. Doesn't it make you wet? It's the biggest prick in the business, darling.' He took her hand and placed it squarely on the front of his trousers. Amelia thanked heaven for the table-cloth. This would have been one photo opportunity that she would never live down. Gostello was panting now. His eyes narrowed menacingly as he watched her face for a reaction.

'Me on top, yeah?' Amelia asked casually.

'Yeah,' panted Gostello. 'You on top. To start.'

'Then lets just settle the bill and go now.'

She had hoped to be able to call his bluff but Gostello couldn't summon the waiter fast enough. He piled a heap of fifty pound notes onto the little silver dish and practically dragged Amelia up the stairs on her nose in his hurry to get his coat out of the cloakroom. Outside, he bundled her straight into the waiting limo and threw himself across her on the wide back seat. The driver raised the glass partition that cut him off from the noise.

'My, you're a foxy little minx, aren't you? A real vixen, with all that red hair. Is it real? Do you have a red bush too?'

'You'll just have to wait and see.' Amelia replied, simultaneously pushing his hand away from the hem of her skirt. 'I'm not about to throw this amazing moment away in the back of a car. I want this to last. To be something that I can treasure in the cold empty nights long after you have gone.'

Gostello raised his head from his contemplation of Amelia's stocking tops for a moment and looked at her with barely focused eyes. His mouth was twisted in a leering smile. She had obviously appealed to his 'better nature', but what was she going to do now?

'I can have any girl I want, Aurelia,' he dribbled frankly. 'But tonight I just want you.'

'And aren't the things you want worth waiting for?'

His hand crept beneath her skirt again. Amelia removed it with surprising firmness.

'You wanna fight?'

'If I have to,' Amelia replied calmly. The chauffeur wound his window down just a little. Amelia caught his eye in the rear-view mirror and he quickly wound it back up again. Gostello persisted. Kissing her roughly all over her neck. His stubble was no doubt bringing her up in a terrible rash. As she threw her head back and sighed with something akin to pleasure, Amelia had a flashback to a room in Las Vegas and a cowboy so scared of a vibrator he thought was a gun he had almost wet his pants. She wasn't sure what she was doing in a car with Gostello but somewhere in the back of her mind she just hoped she'd be able to pull off that kind of stunt twice.

Gostello's home was incredible. A three-storey building just around the corner from Harrods. The chauffeur had to help them get in past the extensive security system of locks and alarms since, by this time, Gostello could barely have opened his flies. He leaned heavily on Amelia as she staggered in the direction of what she assumed would be the sitting-room. The expensive modern artwork on the cream painted walls was in the best possible taste. Such good taste in fact that she didn't suppose for a moment that he had actually chosen it himself.

Amelia pushed open a door to the right of the hallway and spied a double bed. Sod the niceties of seduction. Straight to bed it would be. She man-handled Gostello down onto the duvet and quickly discovered that it was a waterbed as she was unable to stop herself from collapsing on top of him.

'Come here, my darling,' Gostello slurred as Amelia was buoyed away from him on a wave.

'In a minute, in a minute,' Amelia assured him as she managed to hurl herself off the bed and onto the floor where she was able to find her feet again. Amelia hated waterbeds. She was never convinced that they wouldn't burst if you got too excited or electrocute you to death if you turned the heater on. Gostello bounced about in the middle of his king size water sac, looking faintly green.

'Mind if I put some music on?' Amelia asked.

Gostello was only semi-conscious so he didn't protest when Amelia began to hunt around his room. She found the stereo, though it was carefully hidden in an antique-look mahogany sideboard with brass handles that came off when she tried to open it. And at the top of the 'antique' rack of CDs was her own latest release.

'Ha, ha, ha, Mr Gostello, so you don't know who I am,' Amelia hissed.

'What?' he murmured in reply.

She stuck the CD on and turned it up to full volume.

'I'll make sure you never forget my name again. You like this?' she asked him. But Gostello was already asleep. His snoring almost drowned her singing out.

Amelia perched on the edge of the dressing-table and surveyed him. How many women would have given their all to be in this position? Alone in a room with Tracey Gostello. Tracey Gostello flat out on a bed. Huh, he was about as much use as a vibrator without batteries. No, she corrected herself, that was unfair to the vibrator. But what was she going to do with him now? Perhaps she should just call a taxi?

No, sod the expense . . . to Gostello – she would call the chauffeur. But not before she had tidied things up a little bit.

Chapter Eight

FUNNILY ENOUGH, THE chauffeur didn't seem remotely surprised that Amelia wanted to leave so soon.

But this time, instead of climbing into the cavernous and anonymous back seat, Amelia got straight into the front of the car beside him. The chauffeur kept his eyes firmly on the road. Amelia kept her eyes firmly on him. It was unlike Gostello to have employed someone so obviously superior to him in the looks department. Perhaps he had been pissed at the time.

The chauffeur drove in silence. The subtle undulation of his Adam's apple was the only sign that he wasn't in fact a cyborg.

'So, how old are you?' Amelia asked suddenly.

'Twenty-five,' the chauffeur replied, politely.

'Oh.' He was the same age as Guido, Amelia reflected.

'Do you enjoy your job?' she asked next.

The chauffeur hesitated. 'Could be worse,' he replied.

'But it could be better, eh?' Amelia probed. 'Boss a bit of an arsehole?'

'Well . . . I . . . ' the chauffeur stuttered. Was he supposed to agree with her or would that get him sacked?

'Everybody says so,' Amelia replied for him. 'Don't suppose he pays you that much, either. Not when he has to spend so much on antiques,' she added sarcastically. 'What do you really want to do?'

'I want to do this. And to see a bit of the world. I get to go on tour with Mr Gostello.'

'And see the inside of a lot of Holiday Inns,' Amelia sneered. Amelia knew only too well that a rock and roll tour is not the way to see anything other than ironed sheets and minibars.

'You're that Amelia, aren't you?' the chauffeur asked suddenly.

'Yep,' said Amelia. 'That's me.'

They had reached her flat now. The chauffeur pulled the car gracefully up to the kerb, then got out of his side and walked around to open Amelia's door. She placed her hand heavily on his arm as she got out of the car and finally managed to catch his eye. Setting up Gostello had made her very horny and the chauffeur was the most gorgeous man she had seen since touching down at Heathrow. She tilted her head and flashed him her most seductive smile.

Why not?

'Do you want to come inside and make me a coffee?' she asked. Her hand was still on his arm.

'But I'm on double yellow lines,' the chauffeur answered.

'I think I can afford to have it unclamped.'

So the chauffeur followed Amelia into her kitchen and sat nervously on the edge of one of her high wooden stools. Amelia flicked on the kettle and sighed. She seemed to strike fear into the hearts of most men these days. And the only ones who weren't in awe of her were arseholes like Gostello. The chauffeur was playing with a half-empty box of matches that he had found on the breakfast bar, turning it around and around in his fingers, tapping it against the table again and again until Amelia was irritated by the sound of the matches rattling.

'Do you smoke?' she asked. At least that was something quiet he could do with his hands.

The chauffeur took the cigarette she offered eagerly and lit up. Against her manager's orders, Amelia did the same. The smokescreen which gathered between them seemed to make him more brave.

When the coffee was made, they retired to the sitting-room and sat opposite each other on the plush low armchairs. The only light was that which came filtering in through the curtains from the street-lamps outside and the glowing tip of his cigarette. The chauffeur exhaled smoke with a practised air and rested an ankle on the knee of the opposite leg. He said nothing.

'What's your name?' Amelia asked.

'David,' the chauffeur replied. He ran a hand through his short blond hair and narrowed his eyes as he dragged on his cigarette.

'Can I call you Dave?' she asked.

'No,' he told her flatly. 'It's David.'

'Good.' It was the first time he had given a hint of his own free will that evening.

'What can I call you?'

'I thought you knew my name.'

'But it's not your real name, is it?' he asked.

' 'Fraid so.'

'Amelia.' He tried it out. The name dripped off his tongue. As Amelia's eyes had become accustomed to the half-light, she was able to see him smile now. 'Amelia,' he said again. She half expected to see his tongue flick out and taste the air.

'You seemed very shy in the car,' Amelia commented.

'I didn't know what to say to you. Most of the people I drive about don't want to chat and the ones that do chat don't really want me to talk back, just to listen.'

'Like being a hairdresser, yes?'

'Like being a psychiatrist,' David laughed, grinding his cigarette out in an ashtray that Amelia had brought back from Spain. 'Most of Gostello's mates are headcases.'

'That's the music industry for you,' Amelia snorted in reply.

'Yeah, they're all up their own arses. Present company excluded, of course,' he added shyly. 'But they think that getting on ''Top of the Pops'' lifts them out of the real world. Makes them too good for the rest of us plebs.'

'I don't think that's the case,' Amelia retorted. 'In my experience, it wasn't me that changed but the people around me. Sure, I suddenly had a lot of new friends, but equally some of the people I

71

had known for years suddenly became afraid to approach me. It can be an isolating experience, being a celebrity.'

Lost without a cigarette in his hands, David was wiping them nervously on his trousers.

'I mean, it makes it practically impossible for me to approach someone I find attractive without them getting scared.'

'Scared?'

'Yes.'

Suddenly Amelia rose from her chair and fell to her knees in front of David. He couldn't contain a gasp of surprise or embarrassment as she quickly began to unzip his trousers. He was wearing baggy cotton pants, in a shade of green or aubergine which Amelia couldn't quite distinguish in the dark. Amelia fished his semi-hard penis through the slit at the front and greeted it enthusiastically with a long, lascivious lick from its tip to his balls.

David gripped the arms of the chair.

'See, you're terrified of me,' Amelia laughed.

David's penis stiffened automatically, bobbing upright to smack her in the nose.

'Careful,' Amelia laughed.

'No, you be careful,' David squeaked. 'Watch where you're putting your teeth.'

'Sorry,' Amelia ran her tongue along the length of his penis again, then she enclosed the whole of its head in her mouth, gave it a gentle suck then released it.

'Are you still scared?' she asked.

This time, David replied by daring to kiss her straight on the lips.

For a couple of moments Amelia held the penis tightly in her hot hand as she and David kissed. He was a good kisser. His tongue roamed inside her mouth but without threatening to choke her. He held her hair, his hands moving over her scalp until it began to tingle. Amelia loved to be stroked. (If there was such a thing as reincarnation, she intended to come back as a cat.) And each time he stroked her, Amelia echoed the action along the thickening shaft in her palm. David shuddered as Amelia increased the speed of her hand, slicking his foreskin back and forth. The penis was like marble in her hand now and Amelia couldn't help but shudder herself as she thought about taking it inside her and in somewhere other than her mouth.

Suddenly, she tore her lips away from his and dipped her head down between his thighs again. The tip of his penis already glistened with semen that trailed from Amelia's lip like a strand of sugar when she pulled her head away to come up for air. Her eyes smiling, she circled the smooth head with her tongue, savouring the salty sweet taste.

'That feels amazing,' he murmured, as she sucked and licked. His fingers tightened around her narrow shoulders.

Amelia's head bobbed slowly as she dragged the shaft in and out across her lips. She loved the feeling as the glans popped out of her mouth and then sprang upright, begging for more.

But then, suddenly and without a word, David pushed her head away and got to his feet. Before she could protest, he had scooped Amelia up in his arms and was carrying her in the direction of

73

the bedroom. He kicked open the door of her study first, but finally found what he was looking for and pitched Amelia down onto the wide double bed. He leapt on top of her with all the grace of a pouncing Labrador, scrabbling to remove his trousers even as he kissed her all over her face and neck.

Giggling, Amelia helped him to unbutton her shirt, shrugging it off over her head before the last pearly button was unfastened. David hardly bothered to take in the perfect ivory underwear, the underwired, extravagantly lacy bra that held her breasts proudly out in front of her chest and the floaty, matching French knickers. He had ripped them off with barely a thought.

Amelia struggled to position herself more comfortably in the middle of the bed. David threw pillows in all directions until Amelia's head was flat on the mattress. The one pillow that he had left, he placed under her hips to raise them, ready for deeper penetration. A trick he had obviously used before.

Amelia could feel her knickers being dragged down from where they had got themselves stuck around her knees and reached down excitedly to help. He, however, was still in his shirt and tie, though the tie was pretty loose by now. Amelia had only just pulled it free from around his neck when she felt him force his way into her.

She gasped, surprised and excited. He had wasted no time. Without a pause for her to catch her breath, he was powering into her. Pumping and pushing. Grunting and moaning. Pulling her legs this way and that to get deeper inside her still. He folded her legs upwards so that she was open to him but could barely move. His chest crushed her breasts. His breathing was so loud in her ear. Amelia reached back and grabbed for the headboard to stop her skull from banging straight into it as he pounded her body, sending her flying towards the wall with each thrust.

'Slow down, slow down,' she tried to squeal. But it was too late.

David threw back his head with a colossal roar as she felt his penis stiffen inside her. With each jet from his convulsing shaft his body jerked as though he was being electrocuted. Amelia grabbed at his buttocks and held him towards her, trying to force an orgasm out of herself before it was all over. David's face was the picture of perfect ecstasy. His eyes were screwed shut with the effort of it all.

'Aaaaaah!' he cried to the ceiling.

'I'm coming too,' Amelia called. But she wasn't.

'Aaaaaah! Aaaah! Aaah!'

When David had finished he collapsed down on top of her as if his bones had dissolved. Amelia could still feel his penis twitching a little inside. She squeezed her vaginal muscles tightly around him and wrapped her arms across his broad back. He was still wearing his shirt.

After a minute of two, his breathing changed. It was slower and softer. He was falling asleep. Gathering all that remained of her strength, Amelia rolled the heavy body on top of her over to the other side of the bed. Her whole body cried out with disappointment. Then she lay still for a while, unable to fall asleep for frustration, and looked up at the crack in her ceiling with a curious mixture of annoyance and pleasure.

When David emerged from Amelia's flat the next morning, the limo had indeed already been clamped. Gostello, who had obviously got out of bed on the very wrong side, was calling David frantically on his mobile phone, screaming that if he wasn't outside Gostello's front door with the car within the next two minutes he was sacked. David took the final call on the edge of Amelia's bed and when he had turned the phone off, she dragged him back under the covers.

'I guess you're sacked then,' she smiled, reaching towards her bedside table. 'But here's your national insurance.'

From the bottom of her bag she produced a Polaroid photograph.

David took the photo from her and gaped.

It had taken Amelia simply ages to arrange that sheet around David's snoring boss so that he looked as though he was wearing a nappy. But the bonnet she had found in the wardrobe? Now that was a master touch. And who ever leaves an instamatic camera under their bed in these days of scandal and blackmail?

Tracey Gostello deserved all he got.

Amelia scribbled the number of a friendly tabloid newsdesk editor on the back of the picture and handed it back to David with a smile.

'You don't deserve this,' she told him dryly. 'But Tracey Gostello most definitely does.'

Chapter Nine

AMELIA HAD ARRANGED to meet Karis in the Fifth Floor Bar of Harvey Nichols that evening, thinking that they would be able to combine their meeting with a quick tour of the bedlinen department in search of a suitably monogrammed wedding gift. Amelia had explained to Karis when they made the arrangements to meet that she would be looking a little different from usual. She would be wearing a short blonde wig over her long red hair since Tracey Gostello was the only person in London who didn't, or rather who claimed not to, recognise her, and that night Amelia felt like having a little fun incognito. Unfortunately, the wedding had crept up so quickly that it seemed as though that evening's meeting would have to take the place of a proper hen night.

Amelia took up her position on a high stool at the shiny bar and ordered a vodka and tonic, with ice. Karis was characteristically late, or perhaps she was simply unable to recognise her childhood friend without the familiar carrot-top, As it happened, both girls were guilty of not recognising each other. Amelia realised only as she was ordering her third drink that the girl with the chic brunette bob who had spent the last half hour on the far side of the bar was in fact Karis Lusardi of the legendary big hair.

Karis cottoned on at pretty much the same time. They exchanged frantic waves, then they both slipped off their stools and headed for a emotional reunion halfway across the room.

'You look so different,' they both said at once as they crashed together in a tangle of arms and a jangle of bracelets. Then Amelia added, 'At least mine's not permanent. What happened to your hair?'

They had both lost their stools in the excitement of their reunion so they moved across to the wall and leant there together while the suited jerks around them studied their legs from the luxury of the comfortable chairs. Several times Amelia had to say, 'I just can't believe it.' Karis had undergone such a transformation. It was almost as if the girl who liked to take Las Vegas by storm in little more than a pair of red stilettoes had never been outside the home counties in her life. Even the signature red lipstick of her wilder days had gone, to be replaced by a rather muted shade of pink.

'So this is the new Karis,' Amelia sighed. 'You look well, if not very exciting.'

Karis raised her eyebrows. 'Thank you. At least one of us is trying to grow old with some semblance of dignity,' she rejoined. 'Who on earth was that chap you left tied to a bed in New York last week? His pecs were amazing.'

'Oh, him?' Amelia smiled. 'Where did you read about that? Not the *Daily Mail*, I hope? He was just some groupie. I brought him back for my manager, actually.'

'Yeah, right, Amelia. Everyone knows that Rowena likes something with a bit less down below, if you know what I mean.'

'Bisexuality is the latest thing,' Amelia told her.

'Yeah. So I hear,' Karis rejoined with a smile. 'But what about you, Amelia? Anyone special at the moment? Do you still keep in touch with Richard?'

Amelia stared deep into her empty glass. Richard had been the love of her 1994. 'I haven't seen him in a while. Have you?'

'I only ever saw him with you, Amy. He was nice though. Reliable. I always thought that you and he might end up together for good. Kinda hoped you would, anyway.'

'Oh, well,' Amelia rolled her eyes. 'Shit happens. I guess he just couldn't keep up when my career started to take off. Want another drink?' She was desperate to change the subject. 'Then you can bore me with your wedding plans.'

And they really were boring. Karis and Tim were going to marry at the church where Tim had been baptised. Karis would be wearing white, of course, which inspired Amelia to make a crack about the Trades Description Act. The reception would be held in a marquee on the lawn at Tim's father's golf club. And the entire Lusardi clan were flying over from the States to be there in just

79

a couple of days. Amelia wondered idly whether they would be leaving the machine guns at home.

'I wish I had known sooner,' Amelia complained when Karis had finished outlining the best route from the church to the reception, for the fourth or fifth time. 'I feel all unprepared.'

'Yes. But you're here on time, Amy. I can't tell you how much that means to me.'

'But this is a very serious step you're taking. It's the end of an era, Karis. Who's going to be my partner in crime now? We haven't even got time for a decent hen night to finish things off.'

'Oh, well.'

'Oh well? Is that all you can say? The hen night's an important part of the whole thing too.' Amelia persisted. She had decided to play on Karis' love of tradition. 'It's a casting off of your sordid past. Like a final huge feast before Lent.'

'I think I've been feasting on life for quite long enough,' Karis replied. 'Are we going to go and take a look at that linen before the shop closes? I promised Tim that I would be back at nine or so.'

'Nine!' Amelia was outraged. She rolled her eyes in disbelief. 'Don't you dare. This is the last time I will be out on the town with Miss Karis Lusardi and she tells me she wants to go home at nine o'clock. You can't be serious. Not tonight. Let's go to that club we once went to on the King's Road – the one with the table football – and pick up a couple of middle-aged men for old time's sake.'

'Middle-aged men? The very thought disgusts me.'

'But remember what you used to say – "*Tempus*

fugit'', Karis, and ''the effects of gravity are forever''. You aren't telling me that you are going to promise to make love to one man for the rest of your life without checking that you really are sick of the alternatives.'

Karis snorted and ordered another margarita.

'I'll drink this while I think about that question. You want one too?'

Amelia sensed a thaw but continued with her wheedling assault just in case. 'A husband is for life, Karis, not just for Christmas. Just come to one last club with me and I promise I will never ask you to do this again. Never, ever, ever . . . until you're marrying Mr Right mark five, of course.'

'Amelia,' Karis was outraged. 'This marriage is going to be forever. You are mocking true love.'

They argued until closing time and caught a taxi to the King's Road.

When they got to the club, Amelia, still wearing the itchy blonde wig, gave the bouncer the name of her manager and they were waved on past the till. It was a Thursday evening. The club was pretty much empty apart from a small conglomeration of boys in suits at the bar, their ties hanging label foremost from their pockets, and an oriental girl, who appeared to be on her own, chatting earnestly into her mobile phone. She had her Filofax open and was making notes as she talked. She knitted her brows together and chewed the end of her pen. Amelia stood beside her to order a drink. Catching her neighbour's eye, the girl folded up her phone and gave Amelia a friendly smile.

'So many men, so little time,' she quipped.

'I was just saying as much to my friend,' said Amelia.

Karis had chosen a table well out of range of the steadily drinking group of young execs but Amelia angled her chair so that she still had something of a restricted view of a pair of tight buns in pinstripe. Karis took the cherry out of her martini and rolled her eyes.

'This place is such a dump, Amelia,' she complained. 'I can't believe we used to come here for a good time. And that girl on her mobile phone. Purleese! It's so Chelsea. Can't they just leave those things at home?'

'Essential for the busy career girl,' Amelia observed. The girl at the bar had been joined by a man at least twice her age who was wearing a grey suit that had been well-cut for a man half his size. He was peeling a banknote from a tightly rolled wad that he tucked back into his inside pocket without a thought for who saw him do it. The barman nodded politely and bottle of champagne with two tall glasses was placed before him on the bar.

'And are you trying to get me drunk, Amelia, mixing my drinks like this? I had a G & T as well in Harvey Nicks,' Karis was complaining. But Amelia was miles away. The girl at the bar had her head thrown back, laughing loudly at something her companion had just said. She was scribbling a number on the back of a drinks mat for him, then he kissed her gallantly on the hand and left.

Seconds later, the girl left too.

*

'There's not much happening here,' Karis continued to moan. And it was true. Nothing much was happening. The lads at the bar were rapidly losing their charm, not to mention their consciousness. As soon as Amelia had finished her drink, she promised, they would go.

But not home. Not yet.

'This is ridiculous,' Karis told Amelia when she had been persuaded to go yet another 'last ever' club. 'Tim will kill me.'

'If he does then he wasn't worth marrying.'

They had joined a long queue which was snaking towards the entrance of 'Scandalous', a club on the Charing Cross Road which touted itself as the hottest spot in London – if you were visiting on a day-trip from Estonia, that is. Ordinarily, the girls would have walked straight past, but that night the extraordinary length of the queue suggested that maybe they should give it the benefit of the doubt. It took half an hour just to get as far as the door.

Once they were inside, Amelia pushed Karis towards a table right at the edge of the dance-floor. The club was full of women huddled giggling around tables laden with drinks full of umbrellas and cherries and plastic twiddly bits. A couple of girls danced barefoot in the centre of the floor around their shoes and dainty evening bags. Then the DJ put on 'I'm too sexy' and the floor cleared in preparation for the highlight of the evening to begin.

'What's going on?' Karis hissed.

'The cabaret,' said Amelia.

The lights dimmed and dry ice swirled out into the crowd. A gang of girls to Amelia's left began to scream. The song was replaced by a low and dramatic roll of drums. Then, just when it sounded as if the squeals from the audience were about to break glass, the smoke swirled and parted and a man dressed like Dick Turpin leapt down from the DJ box with a mask over his face and a pistol in each hand.

'You're kidding me!'

Amelia and Karis screamed with laughter as the man began to gyrate his hips to the music with all the appeal of their geography master at an end of term disco. He waved the pistols menacingly at the girls in the front row who responded by demanding to see the real thing. He bucked his hips so that his holsters jumped about. He ran the length of the dance-floor, skidding to a halt with his crotch level to some poor girl's nose. One over-enthusiastic member of the audience jumped up and tried to relieve him of his hat. He responded by kissing her roughly on the cheek and sending her into a faint.

'This is ridiculous,' Karis muttered, but Amelia could tell by the look in her friend's eyes that here at last was something that she might actually almost enjoy.

The music changed, though the frantic beat was still the same. The stripper had come to a pulsating halt in the centre of the dance-floor and now drew his tongue lasciviously along the length of his barrel, making Karis snort half her drink back out into her glass. Then he used the end of the barrel to tip back his hat and started to undress – cloak first, with a gaucho's flourish.

He was still wearing his mask. Which was probably a good job, Amelia suggested, since strippers' faces very rarely lived up to anything else they cared to reveal. He was down to his voluminous white shirt already but still waving the pistols. With a lick of his lips he invited a forty-something matron to undo his buttons but she hesitated way too long and he offered the privilege to someone else. Karis was leaning back in her seat now and for the first time that evening she seemed almost like her old self. When the stripper had lost his shirt and was down to his tight leather pants, she stuck her fingers in her mouth and let out a huge whistle, a talent that Amelia had always admired in her best girlfriend.

'He's really not that bad,' Karis breathed graciously as the stripper cantered across to the DJ box flailing his pistols and did an elaborate somersault back into the centre of the floor. It was an opinion with which Amelia had to agree. Sipping her drink, she gazed lazily at the strong square muscles of the stripper's buttocks which flexed to be let out of their hot leather jail. Then, turning towards them, he tensed the muscles of his chest. It was perfect. Not too big and veiny like the pumped up prats of the Eighties strip troupes that women only went to see for a laugh. No, this guy was almost erotic. He wiped a sweaty palm down the leg of his trousers. His mouth was open. He was panting with exertion. He pointed his pistols at the audience again, sweeping them around in a circle. The girls squealed and drew back, as if they knew that this was how he would make his choice.

The pistols stopped on Karis.

He motioned her onto the dance-floor.

Karis rolled her eyes as she got to her feet.

'What a mistake to make,' she said.

Seconds later, Karis was standing just a foot away from the sweaty hunk who had unzipped and kicked off his boots and now stood in nothing but his leather pants and that black velvet mask. Karis's eyes dropped to the flies of his trousers, which were tied, rather than buttoned, with a complicated leather lace. The stripper pointed at his crotch with one of the guns. He was breathing heavily, too heavily to speak.

'OK, Dick,' Karis murmured. 'Do you really want me to do this to you?' She turned once more to the audience and gave Amelia a wink. She reached out her elegant fingers towards the leather lace and took one end between her forefinger and thumb. Then she hesitated. Her eyes met the eyes of the stripper. Behind the mask, she could barely see what colour they were.

The girls in the audience had been whooping throughout the set, but at this point there was a sudden hush. The heavy bass of the dance music had receded and been replaced by an anticipatory drum roll. The spotlight was on Karis now.

Karis was frozen in the motion of reaching for the lace.

Amelia nervously lit herself another cigarette. What was Karis doing? She seemed to be taking forever. Surely her new virginal image didn't extend as far as not stripping a stripper? A murmur suggesting as much rippled quickly through the crowd.

'Come on, Karis,' Amelia shouted finally. 'Get 'em off!'

Karis dropped to her knees. The lace which had been between her fingers was now between her teeth. She was going to take his pants off with her teeth! It was something she had always claimed she could do, but Amelia had yet to see the proof. The crowd roared its approval.

On stage, under the hot lights, Karis struggled to keep a grip on the leather lace as she tugged loose the untidy bow. The smell of the leather filled her nostrils along with another, equally animal smell. She guessed that Dick Turpin must have worn these pants many times before.

As she loosened the fastening, the crowd struck up a slow round of applause, getting faster and faster and faster as Karis drew closer to her goal. Untying the lace was easy once she had unfastened the bow. She worked systematically, pulling first from one end and then the other, her excitement increasing as she saw the trousers begin to loosen and slide slowly down over the stripper's sweaty hips. Her mouth tingled as her lips touched the leather and she noticed that it was tightening unmistakably across his crotch. He was getting a hard-on. She looked up into the bewildered eyes behind the mask.

'It's OK, I won't bite you,' she promised. The stripper raised his pistols above his head and triumphantly fired two caps into the ceiling as his trousers finally slid to the floor.

They weren't the final covering of course, but Karis made quick work of the leopard-skin G-string (which was hardly period, as she would later point out). And soon the most magnificent penis she had seen for a long while sprang out into the spotlight, complete with the little leather strap that was supposed to keep it up when natural enthusiasm couldn't.

The audience set up a litany of ooohs and aahs as Karis got to her feet and started to walk back to her place. She shook her fists above her head like a victor, but she hadn't finished yet. As she neared Amelia, the stripper ran up behind Karis and caught her arm, spinning her around to face him again. Karis gasped as she felt the long dick press hard into her stomach while the lips of the stripper pressed hard upon her face.

The girls around them were screaming and Karis found herself pushed and dragged back onto the floor. The stripper took hold of her hand and wrapped it firmly around his throbbing shaft. Karis was momentarily indignant and tried to pull away but he wouldn't release her hand and soon began to move it for her himself. By the time he had started to sigh with pleasure, Karis had decided to take up the challenge of giving him the best public orgasm of his professional life.

They moved into the spotlight and once again she dropped to her knees. She untied the little leather strap that was holding him so tightly erect. The stripper was bucking his hips to the music. Karis positioned her lips so that the next time he thrust towards her he thrust straight inside her mouth.

Amelia's own mouth was covered by her hand. Even the most disinterested women at the back of the club had pushed forward to see the show upon hearing that some crazy woman was up on stage giving the stripper a real live blow-job. Amelia found herself pushed out of her chair as the crowd surged towards the dance-floor, only to find themselves up against a hoard of jealous bouncers who were supposed to stop things from getting too exciting. Amelia snatched up her friend's handbag for safety and tried not to lose their place at the front.

Karis ran her tongue around the end of the stripper's dick as though it was the most exotic fruit she had ever tasted. She savoured it, as she savoured the applause which burst from the crowd behind her each time she drew a sigh from their dream man.

He tasted of sweat and soap and sex. Smells of the sophisticated man and the animal within him. Then came the taste of salt as Karis licked a path from the base of his balls to the very tip of his penis where a glassy drop of semen had already gathered in anticipation of the arrival of her lips at his most sensitive part.

The stripper's hand held Karis's head as she touched just that drop of semen. She felt his fingers scrunch up her hair as she tantalised the delicate ridge that attached his foreskin to the head. As she licked, she moved his foreskin gently up and down. Her tongue flickered over the eye of his penis one second, the next, she felt that he must be right down her throat. Her lips closed around his shaft. She sucked noisily, leaving lipstick all over him. Above the screaming of the girls and the incessant beat of the music she could hear him sighing more and more loudly. His knees bent slightly, bringing him closer to her. She continued to suck him and stroked at his balls.

'Lick him! Lick him! Lick him!' a gang of girls was chanting.

The stripper had lost his rhythm now. He was no longer bobbing along with the music. The muscles in his thighs were tensed. He was rooted to the spot.

Karis suddenly brought her mouth away from his shaft and ducked, though she was still holding onto the penis which would otherwise have thrashed around like an unattended hose. The sperm shot high, catching the spotlight and almost glittering as it fell in a perfect arc mere inches away from the first row of the audience. The girls at the front stumbled backwards, starting a panic behind them. Karis was oblivious, wiping away a stray shot that had managed to hit her on the side of the face.

At the end of the act, Karis dragged Amelia off to the bar to buy her a Diet Coke for her troubles. 'I'm gasping,' Karis explained. 'That was hard work.'

'You were incredible,' a girl at Karis's left elbow breathed. 'Did they pay you to do that?'

'No, but he should have done,' Karis replied coolly. 'Come on, Amelia. I need a souvenir.'

Over by the loos, the stripper was signing black and white photographs of his best assets for two pounds a time. There were a few poses to choose from. With and without the guns. Karis picked up a snap from a pile which depicted him covering his privates with his pistols and pushed to the front of the queue. Once they had recognised their heroine, no one seemed to mind too much.

The stripper, whose stage name was Rebel Rod, was scarcely looking at the stream of women who asked him to write things like 'love forever' and 'thanks for last night', but when Karis pushed her photo beneath his nose, he recognised at once the beautiful emerald and diamond ring that he had seen on her left hand as she wrapped it around his shaft. He looked up to check that he had remembered correctly. He had. But he wasn't wearing his mask now and Karis looked straight into his slate-grey eyes.

'I'll take this is lieu of a performance fee,' she told him as his hand hovered above the photo. 'Write something original.'

The stripper gulped. Karis didn't take her eyes off his. Amelia recognised the signs of another beautiful man meeting his Nemesis. Sweat. Panic. A moment of slow-motion. Then the stripper smiled, revealing a perfect set of straight white teeth, and began to scribble a note.

'Holiday Inn, Room 605. See you in twenty minutes.'

Karis clutched the photo to her chest, blew Rebel Rod a kiss and left.

Outside, Amelia insisted on seeing the picture and burst out laughing when she read the note. 'Well,' she sighed. 'He's going to be disappointed, isn't he? Now that you're almost a married woman . . .'

Karis was touching up her makeup using the silver mirrored compact from Tiffany & Co. that Tim had bought her for her last birthday. She had fished an ancient red lipstick out of the bottom of her bag and was using it to draw on a familiarly wicked pout.

'I said, he's going to be disappointed, isn't he?' Amelia repeated.

'Maybe he is,' said Karis.

Chapter Ten

THE NEXT EVENING, Karis had to go on 'one last date' with her husband-to-be, and so Amelia found herself in the club on the King's Road again. This time she was alone, still wearing the blonde wig, to which she was actually growing rather attached. It very nearly suited her and it didn't itch that much any more.

As it was a Friday evening now, the club was much busier with people prepared to risk a hangover the next day. However, Amelia soon noticed that the same Oriental girl sat alone at the bar, mobile phone still tucked under her chin, scribbling furiously in her Filofax with the same pained expression on her face. Amelia chose to take the stool next to her and waited patiently for the girl to finish her call.

'It's Friday night. But you can't get away from work, right?' Amelia asked.

The girl smiled at her as she folded up her phone. 'You could say that, yes. I give all my clients my personal number for emergencies and unfortunately there are a few who think that they are always having an emergency.'

'Your clients? Are you a doctor or something?' Amelia knew that she was being naive.

The girl's mouth twitched with the hint of a smile. 'I suppose you could say that too. I'm a health consultant of sorts,' she answered. 'I certainly look after my clients' physical welfare.'

'Nutrition and exercise?' asked Amelia playfully.

'Massage,' the girl added dryly, before turning back to her Filofax. 'It's not really that interesting.'

'Oh no, it is,' Amelia insisted. 'I'm looking for a change of career myself so I love to hear what other people are doing for a living. You never know – you might be able to help me change my life.'

'Right.' The girl was beginning to look irritated. 'But I don't really think so.' She slipped her tiny mobile phone back into her jacket pocket and downed what remained of her drink.

'I'm really fascinated by alternative therapies,' Amelia continued.

'Look, I'm sure you are, but if you must know,' the girl sighed, 'I'm not a therapist, I'm an escort.'

'A hooker?' asked Amelia bluntly.

'That's a little harsh,' came a snorted reply.

'I knew it.'

The hooker tapped a cigarette on the bar and looked at Amelia with cold eyes. 'So, what are you going to do about it? Arrest me for talking on my phone in a bar?' Amelia shook her head. 'You are a policewoman, aren't you? Is that why you wanted to know?' Amelia shook her head again.

'God, you're weird.' The girl lit her cigarette and turned so that she was facing away from her new acquaintance. She tapped her perfectly mani-cured fingernails on the bar in time with the music.

'No,' Amelia persisted. 'I'm not weird but I am interested in doing some of your overtime.' The girl swivelled back to face Amelia again.

'My overtime?' she asked with a sneer.

'Yes. Your surplus work. I noticed you scribbling all your appointments down,' Amelia continued, 'and I figured that you can't possibly have time to see everyone who calls you. You're never off your phone for long enough. I was wondering if you needed a hand. You could take a commission, of course.'

The girl laughed a huge belly laugh. 'If I needed a hand . . .? Well, I must admit that's an offer I've never had before. But I don't think so.' She turned away again to reapply her lipstick before an expensive handbag mirror. 'My overtime?' she murmured to herself. Moments later, however, she turned back and her expression had changed. She was willing to hear more. 'Anyway, in what way do you think you could possibly help me? When my clients call me up, they're looking for something quite specific and it definitely isn't a blonde.'

'I'm not sure but . . . '

Just at that moment her telephone began to ring again. A whispered conversation followed. Meet-ing places. Times. The description of her physical attributes. 'That's extra,' Amelia heard the girl say. 'But of course I can arrange that.' She finished the call, put down her phone and said to Amelia, 'Well, believe it or not, if you really want it, you just got your first job.'

Sue Lee – it wasn't her real name but she didn't want anyone to know that – bundled Amelia into a taxi and took her to a hotel in Knightsbridge where they would be meeting the man she referred to as 'her friend'. Amelia had introduced herself as Natalie and told Sue Lee that she was trying to earn extra cash to put herself through music school. Sue Lee had looked at Amelia in her Hervé Leger dress with a slightly disbelieving smile, but fortunately she didn't question her new colleague's motives further than that.

As they walked through the lobby of the expensive hotel, Amelia felt sure that the girl on reception knew what they were up to, but she turned a blind eye to the visitors and Sue strode on through to the elevators, turning jealous and longing heads with each glimpse of her knee-high suede boots beneath the diaphanous skirt of her expensive dress.

She was dressed from head to toe in black. Around her slender brown arm she wore a thick golden slave bangle. Otherwise, her attire was completely simple. She looked nothing like a hooker, more like a top fashion model on a rare night off.

As they ascended to the client's room in the mirrored lift, Sue checked her immaculate make-up and filled Amelia in on the mission ahead. 'You'll enjoy this, Natalie,' she assured her new friend. 'He's a regular of mine. He usually only has me but tonight he says he feels fit enough for two. He's incredibly cute actually. Very polite. And you might even recognise him. But just keep your mouth shut and do as I say.'

Sue took Amelia's face in her hands and scrutinised her makeup. She wiped away a smudge of mascara on Amelia's cheek with the gesture of a mother tidying up a child. 'Are you sure you want to do this?' she asked, momentarily dropping the hard-girl mask. 'If you don't, you can go straight back downstairs now. I won't mind.'

'No,' Amelia shook her head quickly. Her heart was beating loudly, blood rushing through her ears. 'No, I really want to do this. I wouldn't have asked . . .'

The lift door opened. They had gone to the top floor and one more. A floor that wasn't even marked on the scale that showed you how high the lift had travelled. When they stepped out into the hallway, Amelia recognised with a smile a suite that she herself had once occupied on her second British tour.

'Follow me.' Sue Lee looked unfazed by the opulence of the room they had walked into. 'We need to get ready. The stuff should be through here.'

In a bathroom Amelia remembered to the left of the hall, they found the outfits. Two beautiful tutus hung from the shower rail, exotic creations of brocade and tulle. One white and one black. On the floor beside the bath, there were two pairs of ballet shoes to match. Sue picked up the white dress and held it against her body. 'You had better wear the black one,' she instructed Amelia. 'It looks a bit bigger. You know Swan Lake?' she asked. 'I'm Odette and you're Odile.'

'I'm sorry?'

'The ballet?' Sue explained. 'We've got to do a bit of a dance.'

'Weird.'

'Believe me, this is tame.'

Sue stripped off immediately and was tying the laces of her shoes before Amelia had even reached her own outfit down from the shower rail. Amelia looked at her reflection in horror. She hadn't thought for a moment how she was going to take off her clingy dress without displacing the wig.

'What's up with you?' asked Sue when she had finished dressing and noticed that Amelia had yet to start.

'I . . . I . . .'

'You're not getting cold feet now?'

'No, no, no! It's just that . . .' Amelia took a deep breath. 'It's just that, well –' She smoothed her hand over her wig and gulped. 'It's just that this isn't my real hair.'

Sue Lee laughed. 'Well, thank goodness for that! I thought it looked a bit strange when you first came into the bar but I didn't like to say. Take the wig off then, Natalie, and let's see what you've got underneath.'

Amelia slowly removed the wig and let her own red hair tumble around her shoulders.

'Oh, wow,' Sue breathed. 'That's great. So much better. Why do you want to cover that up?'

Amelia shrugged her shoulders. 'I guess I thought that blondes have more fun.'

'Not necessarily.' Sue continued to tie up her shoes. 'But I'm just relieved that you're not bald.'

Amelia relaxed a little.

It was clear that Sue still had no idea who her companion really was and in retrospect, why should she? Why would a multi-millionairess pop singer go AWOL from her American tour to work as a hooker's apprentice in London? Amelia pulled on the black tutu, which was just a little too small for her, and started to put on her ballet shoes with a rising sense of excitement. From the main room she heard the sound of a man's cough. What would he be like? Rich, obviously. Attractive? She certainly hoped so. The glamour of dressing up had almost suppressed the fear that the client would be just like all the other rich and out-of-condition men who bought Sue drinks in King's Road bars.

'You ready?' asked Sue. She had scraped her dark bobbed hair back into a bun and added just a little more mascara to her beautiful almond eyes.

'I think so,' Amelia told her. Sue gave her the thumbs up sign and led the way out onto the stage.

Chapter Eleven

THE LIGHTS IN the main room were dimmed now but Amelia could still just make out the figure of a man sitting by the window in a high-backed chair. He had on a dressing-gown of some sort and the faint glow from London beyond the window highlighted his narrow feet in their highly embroidered slippers. As Sue and Amelia entered the room, *en pointe* (an occupation in which Sue had obviously already had a good deal more practice), Amelia heard the man sigh.

He pointed his remote control at the stereo and suddenly the room was filled with beautiful music. Sue jumped gracefully across the room and landed with the confidence of a cat. Amelia tried to follow, landing with a little less success, and almost toppling into an expensive-looking Chinese vase. A performer she may have been, but she generally left the dancing to the professionals.

'Don't try anything too fancy,' Sue hissed as they passed each other on tiptoe in the centre of the room. 'This won't take long.' Then, the consummate professional, she flashed a beautiful false smile to her client. The music finished. She glided to a halt like a swan landing on a lake.

Silence for a moment. Amelia teetered on tiptoe, like a child in a game of statues waiting for the music to start again so that she could scratch her nose. Then the clapping started. Just two hands. Polite applause. Sue rose lightly from her position on the floor to take a bow.

Amelia curtseyed shyly and backed up to the wall. Sue had already crossed the room and was perched upon the arm of the client's high-sided chair. He was whispering something in her ear. Sue arched her back and laughed, flashing her smooth, pale throat. Amelia felt a shudder run the full length of her own.

The client rose from his chair and disappeared into another room. Sue walked flat-footed across to Amelia, the net skirt of her tutu waggling like the tail of a little duck behind her.

'I'm going to go in there with him now,' she explained matter-of-factly. 'He thought that he wanted two of us when he called earlier on but now he's not so sure. He says that he's a bit tired. However, you had better stick around – he might have a revival.'

'Oh,' Amelia didn't know whether to be disgruntled or relieved. 'So what should I do now?'

'Just hang on in here. Read magazines. There are some under the coffee table. You could get room service to send up something nice for you to eat, if you like. I won't be long.'

And with that, Sue slipped through the door that the client had used moments earlier. It led to a bedroom, of course.

Amelia sighed. She hadn't even got to see the strange man's face. She flopped down on the high-backed chair and dialled downstairs for a whisky and soda. To be left outside the door.

But Sue had failed to close the door properly and pretty soon Amelia found herself drawn towards the bright gap that led into the bedroom. She was able to walk on the thick carpet in her ballet slippers without making a sound. The room beyond the door was mirrored on all sides, so that even when Amelia had managed to get a good viewpoint, she didn't have a clue whether she was watching the real thing or a reflection.

Inside, Sue sat astride the prone body of a naked man. She was still wearing the white tutu. Her feet were still bound tightly in the uncomfortable pink ballet shoes. She was giggling now as she shuffled backwards along the man's thighs to take his penis in her hand. She stroked the foreskin backwards and forwards almost lazily, talking to him casually as she did so. The client replied in monosyllables that did nothing to dampen her enthusiasm.

'Do you want me to lick you?' Amelia heard her ask.

The man nodded.

Sue shuffled backwards again until she was in a position from which she could reach him comfortably with her mouth. Her bottom was raised in the air and when Amelia looked away from the action to Sue's backside, she noticed with a little shock that the frilly duck's tail knickers were gone. Instead, she was confronted by a pair of tight bare buttocks, between which there nestled a small, dark and shaven slit. Amelia blinked as if she couldn't quite believe it. As Sue sucked with an expression of some enthusiasm at the growing shaft, she performed a weird balancing act so that she could simultaneously stroke her own clit with her delicate long-fingered hand. Amelia watched, rooted to the spot, as she noticed the red painted fingernails appear shyly between Sue's silky light brown thighs. The index finger rubbed at her clit, slowly at first. Then she dragged the finger luxuriously down the length of her glistening slit, to lubricate the little hard nub at its tip. A tiny moan escaped her lips as the client sighed and arched his body upwards with a shudder.

Sue took her mouth away from his penis suddenly, her expression, reflected a thousand times in the mirrored room, concerned.

'You nearly there?' she asked breathlessly.

The client nodded.

Sue leapt up from the bed and positioned herself against the bedside table. Her hands upon it, her legs parted, she was standing on tiptoe with her bottom raised. The client leapt out of bed after her and walked up behind her, holding his penis in his hands and jerking feverishly at its stiff length so as not to lose the momentum he had gained.

'Please, please,' Sue begged, parting the lips of her vagina with her own fingers in preparation and thrusting her bottom back towards him.

The client obliged and rammed his penis home with an enormous grunt. A dozen views of Sue's face quickly changed from pleasure to pain to pleasure again. Her open mouth let out sigh after satisfied sigh as the client began to pump away frantically, hanging onto her hips and using them to bash her body against his. For the first time Amelia noticed his face above Sue's. His eyes were closed. His mouth was twisted into a grimace. His teeth were gritted tightly together as though he was having to make some colossal effort to force his orgasm from his body against his will.

Sue gripped the edges of the bedside table until it shook dangerously each time the client pounded into her. This was no effort for her. She was clearly enjoying every second of it, her groans rising in pitch until they were almost squeaks as the man stopped pumping and withdrew from her suddenly just as he was about to come.

The semen arced gracefully through the air to land with much less dignity on the back of Sue's silly dress. The client held her neck, keeping her head held down until the spasms had stopped and his penis relaxed and hung limp again between his slender legs.

Then Sue turned around to face him. She was licking at her lips. Her eyes were wide and wild with pleasure. She fell to her knees on the fluffy white carpet and greedily sucked the last drops of his come from his softening shaft.

The client's face was softening too. When Sue had finished and was standing up again, he kissed her once, on the forehead, and hugged her slight frame to him almost tenderly. The anger that had been there in his eyes when they were fucking was gone and forgotten. They parted and Sue sat on the edge of the bed to catch her breath while the client counted out a bundle of crisp notes from the top drawer of the chest that Sue had been clinging onto so desperately while they fucked.

The client cracked a joke which sent Sue into spasms. She flopped backwards onto the bed with her legs apart and touched herself as the client continued to regale her with some stupid story. Then, without being told, she seemed suddenly to know that playtime was over, straightened herself up and made for the door.

Amelia skidded back to the chair she was supposed to have been sitting in all the while and tried hard to look nonchalant as she flicked through a car mag.

'Having fun?' Sue asked.

Amelia nodded. 'I was engrossed.'

'In the engine capacity of a Mondeo?'

'Come on,' Sue told Amelia as she duly handed over about a third of the cash to her accomplice. 'He's knackered now. He wants us to go so that he can get to sleep. I'm just going to have a quick shower. You want one too?'

'I didn't really get very messy,' Amelia replied.

She heard the bedroom door click completely shut.

'We can go clubbing now if you like,' Sue continued. 'Sex always makes me feel like dancing.'

'Yeah, OK.'

Sue walked into the bathroom and began to turn the taps.

As Amelia unlaced the painfully tight shoes, she couldn't help thinking back to what she had seen in that room. It wasn't just the sex that had excited her. It was the thought that she had seen that man somewhere before. His face was so familiar. But no matter how hard she tried, she just couldn't quite place it. She had met hundreds of men of his age since she had been in the music business, she reflected. Music men, managers, accountants, photographers, producers, directors. The list was endless and she had Rowena to remember the names for her.

A shudder ran through her. If she recognised him, then he almost certainly recognised her. No. There had been no hint of that. And besides, what was he going to say? 'I hired a brass and it turned out to be Amelia.' His embarrassment would protect her. She just had to hope that he wasn't the vice-president of Midnight Records. Later on, she resolved, she would try and get the truth about his identity out of Sue Lee.

Sue Lee emerged from the steamy bathroom in a completely different outfit to the one she had been wearing when they met in the bar. She gave Amelia the benefit of a twirl in the diaphanous black trapeze-shaped chiffon number that was studded with glittering sequins. 'Isn't this a darling dress?' she asked her audience of one. 'He left it in the bathroom for me. He's always giving me presents. He's the best client I ever had.'

'But who is he?' Amelia asked.

Sue put a finger to her freshly made-up lips, then whispered. 'Can't say now. I'll tell you in the cab.'

Chapter Twelve

SUE LEANED BACK against the black leather seat of the cab and lit up a cigarette. The taxi driver glared at her reflection in the rear-view mirror. The screen dividing him from his passengers was clearly plastered in 'No Smoking' signs. Sue just gave him a friendly little wave.

'I really need this cigarette,' she explained. 'And I'll give him a big tip when he drops us off. You want one?' She offered the box of Silk Cut to Amelia, who declined. Smoking those things would knacker her valuable throat.

'Disgusting habit, I know,' Sue mused. 'But if I ate a chocolate bar every time I had been on the job, which is what I actually feel like doing, I'd be as big as a house.'

Amelia looked at Sue, curled up in the corner of the deep leather seat like a little black bird, and found it hard to imagine someone so petite being even as big as a small garden shed.

'Besides,' Sue continued, 'it's a penis substitute, isn't it? I just have to have something to suck at all times,' she added in an orgasmic kind of way.

Amelia saw the taxi driver raise his eyebrows and tactfully moved to close the communication window and spare his blushes. Amelia always seemed to be protecting men from some rampant girl or other, but she liked Sue. Sue reminded Amelia of Karis – Karis the good-time girl. Karis before the engagement.

'So, where are we going?' Amelia said to change the subject before Sue made a mess of the seat.

'To a private club. Not far from the one where we met, actually. I screw the boss, but he won't be there tonight. He's taking one of my old girlfriends to New York. Can you believe that? The bitch. Just goes to show you should never introduce your attractive friends to your man. Anyway,' she sighed, 'I figured I'd drop in while he's not there and screw his son for free.' Her mouth twisted into a tight-lipped smile.

'And that's revenge?' Amelia asked. 'Sounds more like overtime to me.'

'I know. But he is a rather sweet little thing. Just nineteen. Not the slightest wisp of bum-fluff on his spotty little chin but when he gets an erection its like a diamond drill.'

Amelia blushed.

'I'm sure he's got a friend, if you're interested,' Sue added.

'I'm not sure I'm really . . .' Amelia touched the blonde wig which she had put back on nervously. She had been voted best female artist by *Smash Hits*. There wasn't a nineteen-year-old boy in the

109

universe who didn't know her name and star sign. She had to get out of this. 'In fact,' Amelia continued nonchalantly, 'I think I might call it a day and go straight home now. I just wanted to find out who that client was. He looked vaguely familiar,' she added quietly.

'Well, I'm not going to tell you another thing about that man unless you keep me company.'

'Just his first name?'

'No, not even his initials.'

So, Sue had company when she arrived at the club. The doorman greeted her warmly, kissing her on both cheeks. Amelia was duly introduced as Natalie. The doorman kissed Natalie on the back of her hand with an exaggerated display of chivalry and held onto it for just a moment too long. Amelia panicked, wondering whether he thought he recognised her or whether he just stared at all the girls who came through those doors in the hope that one of them might be melted by his narrow black eyes.

Naturally they didn't have to pay and instead of leaving their coats in the cloakroom, they were straightaway led aside into a private room. Sue draped her wrap on the back of a red velvet-covered chair and sat down behind the desk. She lit up another cigarette.

'This is the big man's office,' she explained as she opened the drawers of the enormous desk one after the other. She came upon one that was firmly locked. 'Shit,' she hissed. 'I bet it's in there.'

'What?' Amelia asked, *faux* naive.

'Guess, sweetheart. You don't think Alphonso got the funding for this place from the Midland Bank do you?'

Sue leaned back in her chair and put her tiny feet up on the desk. She took a drag on her cigarette and puffed out a perfect smoke ring.

'You were good tonight, Natalie,' she told Amelia. 'I couldn't believe it when you said that you wanted to come along. I thought you were a nutter, or a journalist . . . you're not a journalist, are you?' The smile was momentarily replaced by a stony face.

'No,' Amelia protested.

'Jilted wife trying to catch your husband at it with a pro?'

'No.' Amelia shook her head and laughed.

'I didn't really think so,' Sue laughed too. 'Though believe me, it's happened before. But you . . . I think you're more of a voyeur, aren't you, Natalie?'

Sue tipped her head to one side and flicked her cigarette ash into an ornate marble ashtray.

'I saw you watching me through the gap in the door. That room was full of mirrors, you know.'

Amelia gulped and scrabbled for an excuse. 'I just wanted to get some idea of what I might have to do.'

'Did you have a hidden camera?'

'Don't be ridiculous.' Amelia felt herself growing hotter and hotter under Sue's scrutiny.

'I need to know if you did because my client really values his privacy. If our visit tonight was to be leaked to the press by some unscrupulous witness, I might have to send someone round to

111

break your legs.'

'I hope you're joking,' Amelia murmured. Sue's eyes were narrowed. She puffed out another smoke ring.

'Yeah. I am. They'd just break your arms.'

Amelia laughed nervously. 'Well, I did recognise him from somewhere but I can't put a name to the face.'

'Probably for the best.'

'You promised you'd tell me if I came to the club.'

'Later.'

Sue buzzed through to the bar and ordered champagne. Bollinger, of course. And two glasses. When the barman had brought the bottle through, Sue locked the door behind him. She popped the cork of the bottle professionally and poured the sparkling liquid out. Amelia took a sip, squinting as the bubbles went up her nose.

'We could be quite a team, you and I,' Sue told Amelia. 'I think we should raise a toast to it, in fact.'

Amelia raised her glass and chinked it lightly against Sue's own.

Sue was sitting on the edge of the desk now. She drew up one leg so that her shoe rested on the polished wood, scratching the expensive veneer with its narrow metal heel. From beneath the black chiffon skirt, Amelia could see that Sue was still not wearing any underwear. Her shaved pussy was hardly hidden by the wispy shadow of her skirt.

Sue put down her glass and reached out to push the wig off Amelia's head. She laughed when the red hair tumbled out again, then she twisted her fingers in the falling curls and dragged Amelia's head towards hers. Their eyes locked. Amelia felt prickles rising on the back of her neck.

'Well, carrot-top,' Sue teased. 'Let's see how good you are at girl on girl.'

Amelia gasped as Sue fastened her red lips on Amelia's own pink mouth. It was a kiss as hard as any man's. Sue slid from the table and wrapped her arms around Amelia's body, bending her backwards and struggling her around so that suddenly Amelia found that it was she who had her back to the desk.

Amelia collapsed onto it, knocking the Newton's cradle that had probably been there since the Seventies onto the floor with a crash. Sue's mouth was still fastened to hers, forcing her lips apart with a long sinewy tongue that was cold from the chill of champagne.

Amelia fought half-heartedly to free herself from Sue's tiny but strong body which had her pinned down. When Sue sensed that Amelia had given up the fight, she pushed herself upright again, laughing.

One strap of her dress had fallen from her shoulder. The other followed, pushed down by a red-nailed hand. Seconds later, Sue stood almost naked in front of the desk, running her hands feverishly over her own tiny breasts and barely-there curves. She unhooked her stockings and sat down on a chair while she rolled them off over her feet.

Amelia was just recovering herself. She

touched her lip and looked at blood on her finger.

'You bit me,' she accused.

'I'm sorry. I was excited,' Sue replied calmly. She had taken a step towards the desk now and stood with one naked leg on each side of Amelia's lap, wrapping her arms around Amelia's neck like a playful cobra. 'Didn't you like it?'

She fixed Amelia with a challenging gaze. Amelia smiled sarcastically in return, trying not to let her gaze drop to the lithe naked body beneath the face.

'Well, I didn't come if that's what you're asking.'

Sue squealed with excitement, sensing that at least she hadn't received a knockback.

'I'll sort that out for you now, if you like.'

She bent to kiss Amelia on the lips again, rubbing her hairless mound against the silky material of Amelia's skirt. This time, Amelia conceded a little more readily. She had to admit that seeing Sue with her client had been something of a turn-on. Sue exuded a kind of heady sexuality that transcended gender. It was as if she moved between male and female with the changing light.

Sue already had her hand beneath Amelia's dress, pushing it upwards and out of the way. Soon she was helping Amelia to free herself of its tight confines. She draped it carefully across the back of the chair. Amelia was still sitting on the edge of the desk.

Sue took a sip from the champagne glass that had survived their grapple so far and handed it to Amelia. Sue's straight black hair fell across her

114

face with graphic precision, cutting in half the red gash of her mouth, which was by turns snarling and pouting as she removed Amelia's underwear like a locust stripping petals from a rose.

'You have a great body,' Sue murmured when the undressing was complete. 'I noticed that when you were dressing at the hotel. Such full breasts.' She placed a kiss on each of the gentle curves. 'I haven't got anything to speak of,' she indicated her own flat chest. 'I could do the ironing on this.'

Amelia reached out curiously to touch her.

'Kiss them anyway,' Sue begged her new lover. 'Lick them. Suck them for me.' She leaned forward over Amelia's face so that the tiny breasts hung down like two little pyramids of pink. Tentatively Amelia lifted her head to the proffered breasts and flicked out her tongue. The delicate rosy nipples stiffened immediately at the merest suggestion of Amelia's caress.

'Harder than that,' Sue complained. She put a hand beneath Amelia's head to pull it closer to her breast and thrust one of the quivering buds into Amelia's mouth again. 'Bite it,' she commanded. Part of Amelia's mind fought against the suggestion but she gently and obediently closed her teeth together on the stiff little bud. 'Harder,' Sue rasped again. 'Harder than that.'

As Amelia concentrated her attention on the breasts, Sue's hands had crept lower. 'No, don't,' Amelia pleaded as she suddenly realised the turn events were taking. 'I really don't think I want . . .'

'What?' It was too late. Sue had already broken

down her defences. Her slender fingers brought Amelia up in goosebumps of nervous desire as they stroked her into submission.

Amelia closed her eyes as Sue's fingers tangled in her pubic hair, waiting for the inevitable to take place. The touch of those soft fingers on her clitoris made Amelia bite her lip and sent arrows of tingling electricity all over her body. Pinching and massaging her, Sue kissed Amelia again, thrusting her tongue inside Amelia's sweet mouth as her fingers echoed the action down below.

'Aaaaah!' Amelia broke away from her lover's mouth and threw back her head. 'Don't do that.'

'Sssssssh, calm down,' Sue whispered. 'You're so nice and warm inside. So wet. You're enjoying this. Don't tell me that you're not.' A peculiar tingle ran down Amelia's spine at these words. 'Just lie back and relax, Amelia. I'm going to make you come all over me . . .'

Automatically Amelia raised her hips a little and braced her feet against the floor. Sue smiled her approval and now licked her lips as she contemplated the task ahead and ducked her head down between Amelia's thighs.

With the very first flick of her tongue Sue found Amelia's clitoris. She bucked her hips upwards with the surprise. While they were raised like that, Sue grabbed her lover's buttocks and used them to lift the girl still further, so that she could more easily reach her target. Her tongue moved slowly at first, up and down the shiny shell-pink of Amelia's vulva, tantalising her stiffening clit. Sue's eyes were fixed on Amelia's all the time.

Every cell in Amelia's body was beginning to vibrate at her touch. She felt giddy, as if she was hesitating at the very top of a roller-coaster ride before that fall that makes you weightless. The fall that puts your heart in your mouth.

'You've just got to let go,' Sue commanded. 'Or it'll never happen. Let go, Natalie. Just let yourself come. I can feel you're almost there. I can smell you coming.'

When Sue looked up again, she was wet from her nose to her chin. It wasn't all saliva. She returned to her frantic licking. Amelia's hips bucked even higher again, as if to drive Sue's tongue into her. Her eyes tightly shut, Amelia grasped at the jet-black head bobbing between her legs, forcing it further between her shaking thighs. Sue wouldn't have to ask Amelia to come again. Suddenly Amelia's body took over. Every muscle was tensing and relaxing, tensing and relaxing so strongly and so quickly, it was as if she had been plugged into some peculiar source of electricity.

Amelia grasped the hard edges of the desk and clung to them desperately as the excitement within her prepared to break loose.

'Oh, oh, yes!' Amelia bucked upwards so hard that Sue reeled backwards momentarily, losing her balance where she squatted on her high spike heels. But Sue soon regained her composure and was back again like the tide relentlessly making for the shore She continued to lick, long, hard, strokes, right up until the very last moment, when Amelia felt that she was about to pass out and she flooded Sue's face with salty sweet come.

When Amelia had finished shaking, and sat upright again on the ransacked desk, Sue sat down beside her and kissed her gently on the lips. Amelia was sure she could taste her own juices on the tip of Sue's wicked tongue.

'Was that good?' Sue asked.

Amelia nodded in reply. She closed her eyes and breathed in deeply.

'Too good,' Amelia sighed.

Sue looked her straight in the eye. 'But you know that if we're going to be a team, I need to know that you can do the same for me.'

'Is that a challenge?' asked Amelia.

'I suppose it could be. Go ahead.'

Sue reclined nonchalantly on the hard desk, her legs parted, waiting for Amelia to come between them.

'What are you waiting for?' Sue asked, eyebrows raised.

Sue slid forward so that her spike heels touched the floor and her shaven sex was at the very edge of the desk. She reached out her hand and twisted a little of Amelia's long red hair between her fingers, using it to pull her over. Sue's pouting labia were red and wet with desire, communicating a message to Amelia which she couldn't ignore now.

Amelia pulled up the boss's chair and settled herself between Sue's legs.

'Nice touch,' Sue smiled as she placed a vicious heel on each of the padded leather arms. 'Very nice touch.'

Amelia gazed at the picture before her. The sweet scent of soap and shower gel drifted towards her from Sue's hot and quivering thighs. Amelia hesitated. Sue moaned and ground her buttocks down against the desk, pressed her feet down hard against the arms of the chair until the muscles in her legs were clearly defined. Sue traced her own labia with her fingers, parting them slowly. Showing pink. Amelia wrapped an arm around each of the legs in front of her and leaned forward into position.

Sue sighed contentedly and her hips rose slightly from the desk. She couldn't wait for Amelia to begin. The musky female aroma that Amelia had smelled on her own fingers after masturbating was rising gently towards her from Sue's vagina, enticing Amelia further down. Taking Sue's slender hips in her shaking hands, Amelia made the first hesitant dive, stretching out her tongue to its full pink, hard length, licking and then penetrating, coaxing a smile from Sue's perfect red mouth.

Tasting that familiar perfume and being delighted by it, Amelia licked and licked, faster and faster in response to the excited moans which came from the girl on the desk. Sue reached her arms behind her head and writhed on the blotter, sending a pile of papers scattering onto the floor. Amelia continued to lick and suck at the tiny hardened clitoris, now more confidently and harder until Sue's hands clutched her head and she cried, 'I'm going to come! I'm going to come!'

Up and down, up and down, Sue's hips bucked, so that Amelia felt her tongue was fucking the girl. Then Sue pushed Amelia away from the centre of her pleasure and pulled her up from the chair so that they were level again and their mouths touched.

Sue wrestled Amelia to the hard carpeted floor, flipping her over onto her back with surprising strength. She ground the mound of her pubis against Amelia's, and they rocked back and forwards, Sue's hands grasping for Amelia's breasts, Amelia's hands sweeping up and down Sue's back, streaking her skin with lines that went white and then red. Sue was moaning, sighing, desperately clutching her lover's body harder and harder to her own. Amelia put just one finger into Sue's vagina. The muscles there were opening and closing like a crazy flower as Sue soaked her hand. 'I'm coming, I'm coming,' she continued to scream at the top of her voice while Amelia pumped her finger in and out of the pulsing vagina and could hardly believe what she had done.

Amelia's pulse had barely returned to normal by the time Sue had dressed again. Sue brought the jewel-encrusted mirror out of her handbag and carefully dabbed powder on her cheeks and her nose. She offered Amelia the compact too, but it was in the wrong shade for Amelia's lily-pale skin.

'I'm going to go home now,' Sue told her. 'But you can stay here for as long as you like. Just mention my name and the drinks will be free.'

'Thanks,' Amelia replied. Though she didn't think she would be hanging around for too long after Sue had gone. Sue smoothed an eyebrow back into place and clicked the compact shut.

'So,' Amelia hesitated. 'Do you think we might be able to work together again?'

'I don't see why not, partner. I'll be working again tomorrow night. I'll meet you at the same time in the same place if you like?' Sue twisted a key and opened the door.

Amelia nodded. 'Tomorrow? I'll be there.' Then she remembered and called, 'Who was that guy?'

But Sue wasn't about to let her know. She just waved goodbye and walked away. Amelia smiled and nodded to herself. Sue was a true professional all right.

Amelia took a last look around the grubby little office and picked up her bag. She checked in her handbag mirror that her wig was on straight. What a crazy night it had been so far. Rowena would have thrown a fit. But the danger had turned Amelia on so much. The unpredictability of Sue's kind of work was probably the most attractive part of it.

Just at that moment, from somewhere in the room Amelia heard a telephone burst into life. She swivelled around in the direction of the ringing. But it wasn't the phone on the desk. Amelia picked up the handset just in case and got nothing but a dialling tone. The ringing continued. Amelia looked beneath the desk and quickly found the source. It was Sue's mobile phone. It must have somehow been kicked there while she and Sue had tangled on top of it.

It continued to cry shrilly, like a child ignored by its mother. Amelia bent down slowly and picked it up. She pressed the little green talk button and took a deep breath.

'Hello,' she said.

'Hello,' echoed the caller at the other end of the line.

There was a long pause. Then the caller spoke again.

'Are you busy tonight?' he asked.

'No,' Amelia replied. 'I'm not.'

'Are you working?'

'I wasn't planning to.'

'Oh.' The caller sounded disappointed. Amelia felt her heart quicken against her rib-cage. The caller didn't seem to have noticed that she wasn't Sue.

'I'm sorry,' he said suddenly. 'I don't do this very often. What can I do now? Should I make an appointment?' He laughed nervously.

'I'll see if I have a window in my diary,' Amelia laughed equally nervously in reply. He had a nice voice, this caller. Very cultured. Amelia let her mind wander and imagined him to be in his forties. A successful businessman, with elegantly greying hair. The caller cleared his throat as Amelia made him wait for her to make up her mind.

'Where are you?' she asked.

'I'm in Hampstead,' said the caller.

Amelia made a mental calculation of how long it would take her to get to him, do the business and get back to her own place for some beauty sleep. Karis would be getting married in the morning. Amelia had to be at the church for eleven. She glanced at her elegant Cartier Tank watch. It was half past three already. To do this job would be madness . . . but . . .

'Hampstead,' she repeated. 'I can be there in

122

half an hour.'

She scribbled down the directions and used Sue's phone to call a cab.

A little more than half an hour later, Amelia stood on the pavement outside the tall house in Hampstead and chewed her lip. The sudden rush of daredevil bravery she had felt in the club was wearing off already. A light shone in a room upstairs, silhouetting the tall figure of a man which passed the curtains from time to time. This was very different from the job in the hotel. Amelia was suddenly very aware that she was completely on her own. There was no possibility that this guy was going to be too tired to take her on. What if he was disgusting? What if he wanted her to do something terrible? What if this man was dangerous?

Amelia began to walk back down the road. The cab she had caught this far was long gone, but she would probably be able to hail another one easily enough at the Tube station. Then, inexplicably, at the bottom of the road, she froze. She looked back at the tall house, dark and slightly sinister in the shadow of the trees. At the one lighted window, the figure of a man now stood, hands on the windowsill. He was looking down the road towards her. He knew that she had come this far.

Without knowing why, Amelia turned again and walked back in the direction of the caller's front door.

He opened the front door as she walked up the path. Behind him, a normal enough looking house. The hall walls were painted yellow and hung with old prints from *Vanity Fair*. A pile of coats was draped across the knob at the end of the stair-rail. Not all of them were men's coats. This was a family home.

'Coming in?' the caller asked. Amelia recognised the voice on the phone straight away. She stepped into the hallway and let the door close behind her but she stayed on the doormat, frozen to the spot.

This was not what she had imagined.

The caller stood in front of her, running his fingers nervously through his thick, dark hair. He was about as old as she had imagined. In his forties, maybe forty-five. But he was in far better shape than she had hoped. He was wearing a pale blue shirt, open at the collar, tucked into a pair of dark blue denims fastened with a thick leather belt. His feet were bare. Amelia glanced down at his long brown toes. He ran the other hand through his hair and made some kind of hopeless gesture with a shrug of his shoulders.

'Through here, I guess,' he said, ushering her through into a sitting-room to the right of the hall. Amelia found herself standing nervously in the centre of another mat – though this time it was an expensive carpet – clutching her handbag in front of her stomach. She took in the decor. In this room, the walls were dark red and covered in yet more prints and paintings. Shelves to either side of the fireplace were piled high with books on DIY and history. Along the mantelpiece were arranged a number of small framed photographs. A couple of children. A smiling woman. A soft looking dog. Amelia strained but wasn't sure that she could see a snap of the man.

'Drink?' the man asked.

'Not unless you're having one,' Amelia replied. He wasn't.

'Then I guess we might as well go straight upstairs.'

'I'm Natalie,' Amelia told him as they climbed the long staircase to the first floor. The man turned to look down at her and smiled, but he didn't tell her his own name. He pushed open the door to a bedroom. In the middle was a wide double bed, piled high with pillows and covered with a dark red bedspread.

Amelia slipped off her coat and let it hang from the back of a velvet cushioned chair. As she did so, she suddenly remembered her wig and touched her hand to the synthetic hair. What was she going to do about that? She turned towards the dressing table mirror on the pretence of checking her make-up, to see how the wig had faired the cab journey. It was still OK. She would just have to avoid getting energetic.

While she checked her hair, the man had positioned himself on the end of the bed, feet flat on the floor. He had taken off his trousers and his crisply ironed boxer shorts, but he kept the shirt on.

'Just a blow-job,' he told her.

Thank goodness for that, thought Amelia, as she knelt before him on the floor.

She lifted the bottom of the man's shirt out of the way and looked at the penis which lay curled and lifeless in front of her. Gently she took it in her hands, holding it between them, as if she was trying to resuscitate it with the warmth of her palms. The man leaned back, supporting himself with his arms. Amelia looked up into his face, but his eyes were already closed.

This was so bizarre. She had never got this close to a man without at least knowing his surname. What was she supposed to do? Act like she did this all the time?

She bit her lip and began to work on him as she would have worked on any man that she had dated before. Carefully she pulled the penis to its full length and slipped the very tip between her soft lips. Holding the foreskin back, she flicked her tongue backwards and forwards over the tiny eye. Then down a little further, until she was flicking the ridge of skin that attached the foreskin to the shaft. The man exhaled noisily. His shaft began to stiffen. Amelia was doing all right.

He smelt clean, thank goodness. As she licked his shaft from tip to balls, she caught a whiff of soap from his pubic hair. His stomach was flat and very firm for a man of his age. His thighs too were well-muscled. Well-kept. As the penis was standing up on its own now, Amelia allowed her hands to roam over his beautiful legs for a while. The feel of his hairy thighs beneath her hands was almost a turn-on for her.

Then the shaft twitched powerfully and Amelia had to take hold of it again to stop it from banging against her sharp teeth. She set to working the foreskin back and forth with her hand once more as she licked him.

This time, she sneaked a look at his face. His eyes were still shut. His neck glistened with sweat above the crisp collar of his shirt. Amelia ran her fingernails over his balls. The client's stomach tensed and he moaned with pleasure. Amelia took her mouth away from him and smiled at the power she had right now.

She moved her hand faster to hurry the moment on. When she felt that he was almost ready, she lowered her mouth to the head and flickered her tongue across the glans. She wondered how it felt to him. When someone did that to her clitoris, she felt as though they had lit a slow burning fuse that was impossible to put out. The man swallowed hard and pressed his feet down against the floor. Amelia sucked him right between her lips, surrounding him with the soft, warm wetness of her mouth. She increased the pressure of her tongue against his shaft and continued to fondle his balls. Then she scored a hard path up the inside of his thigh with her nails. He drew breath sharply. His moans were rising towards the high ceiling of the beautiful room. His hands left the bed and he slumped forward on top of her, making it difficult for her to move any more.

But she didn't need to. She felt his shaft stiffen against the roof of her mouth, the muscles contract and then relax, pushing the first jet of come deep into her throat. She continued to suck, swallowing at the same time. The body on top of her was jerking and sighing. His hands grasped the silky material of her dress, almost roaming around to her breasts but then they went loose again and relaxed as though they were lying on a piece of wood rather than a woman.

When he had finished, Amelia sat back on her heels and wiped clean the corners of her mouth.

The man lay prostrate on the bed with one arm slung over his eyes. With the other he waved Amelia in the direction of a white envelope on the bedside table. He didn't say a word.

So the job was over before five in the morning. Amelia took the money she had been offered and rolled it into a tight tube before stuffing it in her pocket. She walked towards the Tube station straightaway because she didn't want to hang around in that chilly house while she waited for a taxi. Once outside the station she gave that evening's earnings to a young girl who was curled up in a sleeping bag with a manic-looking dog.

The girl hardly blinked as she took the five twenty-pound notes from Amelia's hand. She had barely woken up and probably thought it was just a dream.

Amelia sank gratefully into the back seat of a mini-cab that sped her back home. All she needed now was her bed. But it was as they turned into her street that it struck her. Sue must have a string of incredible clients, because, like the man in the hotel, Amelia was suddenly aware that she had seen that man in Hampstead somewhere before. A glance at an album cover would confirm it as soon as she got inside.

Amelia rushed straight to her vast and dusty collection of old vinyl 33s. What was the name of that album? She racked her brains as she flicked through cover after cover, finding that every other record was one that she would have to play that night for old times' sake. After four hours, her search interrupted by having to dig out a record player and spin more than a few discs, she found it.

'Messages at Midnight' by the Devonfield Experience. She flipped open the gatefold cover excitedly and there he was, in black and white. Twenty years younger, in a tux and tastefully airbrushed, but it was definitely him. Amelia still couldn't believe it.

She murmured to herself in a amazed whisper, 'I just sucked Tony Devonfield's cock.'

She plucked Boney M off the turntable and stuck 'Messages at Midnight' in its place. It had been one of her favourite albums, nearly fifteen years before, though even then it was a good five years out of date. Amelia had inherited the album from her eldest sister, who had just moved on to punk.

Carefully Amelia picked up the needle and let it drop back onto the shiny black grooves. For a while, there was nothing but the crackle of static and dust, but then . . . Oh wow. A delightful shiver ran across Amelia's back as the familiar chords struck up once more. She clicked her fingers through the introduction to the first song and joined in with the lyrics at exactly the right time. Yes. This was one of the best albums she had ever owned.

Amelia got to her feet and danced around the dusty record player until the end of side one.

By the end of side two, she was lying on the floor, listening to two particular tracks again and again and again. 'Never do it' and 'Questions of Love'. They were perfect, those two tracks. Amelia dissected the tunes and broke them down into sounds. Perfect pop. This was what she wanted to be able to play. This was how her next album should sound. She sat up thoughtfully and set the needle to go one more time.

It was easy.

She could ask Devonfield to produce her next album. What a coup! Rowena would be very surprised.

But at the same time, it wasn't that easy.

Tony Devonfield had been one of the most popular artists of his generation, outselling the rest of the charts two to one ... but he had disappeared almost as suddenly as he had risen to fame. He hadn't released an album since the end of the Seventies. People said that he had fled to the countryside and become a hermit. He had given one last interview to the *NME* saying that he would never record a single note ever again.

But that was twenty years ago, Amelia told herself as she slipped the disc back into its white paper inner sleeve. He had had a little while to change his mind about that career decision. Amelia decided that she would go and see him before she went back to the States. She would run the idea past him. What a glorious way to come out of retirement! How could he possibly refuse?

But first, she had to go to Karis's wedding. And, having wasted half the night listening to old tunes, she had time for just half an hour's sleep.

Chapter Thirteen

TO HER ETERNAL relief, Amelia had managed to
get out of being bridesmaid, pleading the
impossibility of getting a grand enough dress in
time. And in any case, Amelia was too unreliable
a timekeeper these days to be trusted with such
an important position in the bridal party. It was a
good job too because, as it happened, Amelia
arrived at the church at the same time as the
bride's mother, screeching into the car-park in a
hired blue Renault Clio. Karis's elder brother
Louis, who was standing outside the church door
as an usher, quickly pinned a flower to Amelia's
pale green jacket as she passed inside. Amelia
was relieved to notice that he had left the violin
case at home.

'You doing all right?' Louis asked without
moving his mouth.

'Yeah, Louis, thank you,' Amelia replied. She
smiled fondly as Louis fussed about in an attempt
to straighten up her wilting corsage. She had had
a big thing for Louis once. That was when she

was just a gawky teenager and Louis was a twenty-something smooth guy with a pretty special car. Now he was growing out of his looks a bit. But there was still something there. That legendary Italian charm.

As Amelia settled into her seat on the bride's side of the church, she found herself thinking of Louis again, but this time his face was confused. With Guido's perhaps? Amelia shuddered in the nicest possible way as she had a flashback to that last night in New York. A thought of her face pressed against the cold window that looked down onto Central Park as he powered into her from behind. The hot, wet tickle of his come as it dribbled down the inside of her leg.

All eyes turned to the back of the church as the organist struck up the wedding march. Amelia hadn't even had time to open the service sheet and now Karis was coming down the aisle.

'How's the dress? How's the dress?' the ancient Lusardi aunt at Amelia's side pestered for a résumé of the view she was too wizened and short to see.

'It's beautiful,' Amelia breathed. And indeed it was.

As Amelia might have expected, Karis had gone the whole damn hog and as a result her dress took up most of the aisle. It had a tight, beaded bodice that clung to her generous curves like a second skin. Then the skirt billowed out from the narrow waist like the petals of a late summer rose held upside down. Her face was covered by the demurest of veils . . . but Amelia still caught Karis wink as she walked on by.

'The bouquet's for you,' Karis hissed.

Amelia hissed back, 'Thanks.'

It still hadn't hit her, even when seeing Karis in the outfit, that this was really happening. That the Karis who walked out of the church would be an honest woman, theoretically. The elderly aunt was dabbing a handkerchief at her eyes.

'She looks so much like her mother,' the old woman wailed.

'She does, doesn't she,' said Amelia.

Karis would have loved to hear that.

The organist stopped playing. Karis and her father had reached the altar. The handsome, burly bridegroom gently pushed back her veil. It was a scene straight from a fairy-tale . . .

Until the bride and the best man caught each other's eye and the whole congregation reeled in horror as Karis shrieked 'Ohmigod!' and fell in a faint to the floor.

Well, the last thing she expected was for the best man at her wedding to be Rebel Rod.

But the wedding went ahead when the bride came round again. Apparently, Karis had always been of a nervous disposition and what with the excitement of the day and everything it was hardly surprising that she had a bit of a swoon . . . And didn't Rod look the absolute image of Cousin Tony, the cousin on her father's side of the family who had accidentally gone diving off the Brooklyn Bridge in 1984. That was the trouble. Tony had been Karis's favourite cousin. She must have thought she was seeing a ghost or something . . . And since Rebel Rod's own fiancée Melanie was in the congregation, he didn't exactly venture to suggest otherwise.

However, Karis was still almost as white as her dress at the beginning of the reception, which was held in a pink and white marquee on the golf club's front lawn. Rebel Rod got hurriedly plastered on buck's fizz and they had to cut his speech altogether by the time the jokes about everybody having known the bride beforehand had been edited out. Amelia, sitting at a table full of Karis's siblings, looked on her best friend's discomfort with a certain amount of pleasure. After all that business about Amelia getting first refusal on the bouquet, Karis had thrown it straight in the direction of her cousin Louisa instead.

'You having a good time?' Louis asked for the fifth time that day.

'Yeah,' Amelia nodded again, as she passed him her glass for a refill.

'I still can't believe it,' he confided in her. 'My little sister. My sweet little sister Karis. Seems like only yesterday when you two were playing together in her room at our house. What was it you played all the time, Amelia? Doctors and nurses, I guess?'

'Sort of.' Amelia sipped at her champagne with a smile. Most of the time they hadn't been in that room at all. They would have shinned down the drainpipe and gone in search of doctors for real at the local medical school .

'You've grown up now, though,' Louis continued in a whisper. His hand had crept beneath the table and onto her silk-stockinged knee. 'And now that you're all famous and stuff I don't s'pose you got much time for your old friends any more.'

'On the contrary,' Amelia replied with a demure smile as Louis ran his rough hand up and down her leg, doubtless skagging her stocking as he did so. 'I feel as though some of my friends have changed their feelings towards me.'

'I still feel the same about you,' Louis confided.

'You do?' said Amelia, surprised. But what did that mean? Did he still think she should get braces and some treatment for her acne?

'I always really liked you, but, you know, you were my little sister's friend. I couldn't be seen to be setting myself on you. It wasn't done . . . The boys would have had my guts . . .'

'For garters?' Amelia murmured as Louis's fingers found hers. 'Well, I never would have guessed . . .'

Louis leaned in close. Amelia could feel his breath hot on her ear and imagined it misting up the diamonds in her earrings. 'But you look even better now,' he murmured. Amelia felt a centipede with needles for feet run right up her spine at a gallop. Louis squeezed her knee. After half a bottle of bubbly, he still looked pretty good himself. Amelia remembered watching him change through his bedroom window from the security of Karis's tree-house. She remembered his twenty-year-old chest, hard and broad, nut-brown and with the first smatterings of curly black hair. Amelia looked down at the back of Louis's hand which rested on her thigh. Wiry black hairs crept out from the edge of his cuffs. His nails were clean though, which was something they had never been when he had spent all his spare time in the garage working on his very first car.

'Ladies and gentlemen.' Karis's father was trying to get everyone's attention by banging a wine glass with his spoon.

The bride and groom were about to cut the cake. Louis and Amelia followed the other guests across the marquee to form a rough semi-circle around the happy couple. To the left of the newlyweds with their nervously fixed smiles, Rebel Rod was bickering with Melanie. He was so drunk that Amelia doubted he would be able to get a prodigious hard-on even at gun-point that night.

Karis and Tim drove the knife into the cake, almost bending it on the rock-hard icing. It had been made by Karis's Aunt Maria and Amelia wondered when they would hit the file. Polite applause rippled around the room. Only Louis wasn't clapping. But not because he didn't approve, rather because he had one of his hands on Amelia's shoulder and the other on her tiny backside. When the guests began to move back to their tables to make one last attempt at drinking themselves under them, Louis steered Amelia outside into the gardens by her buttocks.

'Come outside,' he whispered.

He was doing the steering.

'Do I have a choice?' she asked.

It was a fine night for September, thank goodness. Torches of dripping wax lit up the paths between the trees and late living moths fluttered about drunkenly in their glow. Louis and Amelia walked without saying a word until they were just out of sight of the marquee. Then he dropped her hand, which he had been holding politely, and clenched her to him suddenly for a kiss.

'Louis, Louis,' Amelia murmured as she tried to regain her foothold in her slippy strappy shoes, but to no avail. She was entirely at his mercy now. In fact she wasn't sure that she had either of her feet on the ground at all. Louis swayed her from side to side until she felt dizzy, kissing the life out of her. Finally Amelia gave up battering his thick back with her little fists and let him carry on. It wasn't quite how she had imagined it would be, sitting in that tree-house eleven years before, but it wasn't that bad at all.

Louis came up for air. Amelia whipped out her compact to inspect the damage to her lipstick.

'Did I hurt you?' Louis asked.

'No,' said Amelia as she smoothed her eyebrows. 'But that was quite some kiss.'

'It represented fifteen years of suppressed desire,' Louis announced.

Amelia was taken aback. Louis was the last person she would have expected to suppress anything.

'In that case.' She wrapped her arms languidly around his neck again. Louis grunted softly as he nuzzled into Amelia's Chanel-scented shoulder. His hands crept onto her bum, rucking up her pale green skirt until her suspenders were on full show.

'Hang on a minute. Someone might see.' Hearing voices nearby, Amelia edged Louis back into the flower-bed and further into the cover of the trees that edged the golf course. As she moved, she felt one of the clips on her stockings ping free and let out a giggle. Louis was laughing too as he swung her around until she was leaning against the rough bark of a nice big tree.

'Oh, Louis,' she sighed as he leaned heavily against her. She could already feel his hard-on through his neat grey trousers. Panting, she slid her hand down between them until it rested lightly on the pulsating shaft.

Louis groaned and pulled Amelia's skirt up again until she felt the bark against her bare thighs. She moved to try to stop it from scratching but Louis was barely giving her room to breathe. He was moving up and down now, with his legs on either side of her right thigh, using it like a cat uses a scratching post to deal with his fifteen year itch. His breath on her ear became more and more ragged. He was sighing her name with every other breath.

'Louis, Louis,' she murmured in reply, running her hands up and down his back beneath his jacket. She slid her hands round to the front and began to unfasten his tie. Louis slipped off his jacket and let it fall to the ground. Without a word he pushed her gently down on top of it, making sure that she didn't get her skirt dirty, though her stockings were already in shreds and the spiky heel on one of her shoes was feeling distinctly shaky.

He began to fumble with his zip. But the unfamiliar formality of the hook fastener at the waistband of his trousers was giving him real trouble. Amelia reached out to help him. Louis put his hand up her skirt again, rubbing at her clitoris though the soft silk of her panties.

'I can't believe we're actually doing this,' Amelia murmured. Louis was dragging her panties off now. They were already around her knees. He bunched her skirt up around her waist and began to kiss her stomach. His penis, freed from the smart grey trousers and his boxers underneath, was tapping against her leg.

Amelia slid down the floor towards him, arranging her legs on either side of his strong hips. Louis still fumbled at her vagina, sliding a finger carefully in and out. Amelia shivered with anticipation. She needed something bigger. She needed something more. She took Louis's penis between her hands and began to guide it towards her.

They still kissed with tiny pecking kisses as he nudged at the entrance to her desire. Amelia parted her lips with her fingers, making more room. Louis drew himself up on his arms and positioned himself to plunge in. Amelia braced her feet against the floor and pushed upwards at the same time.

'Ooooh!' she moaned happily as she felt her body give way to the insistent pressure of his knob against her labia. She felt herself being stretched and sighed. She grasped Louis's buttocks and pushed him in further. This was exactly how she had always imagined it to be, though she hadn't expected their coming together to take so bloody long.

Louis groaned with excitement. For him too, this was the fulfilment of a long held wish. He moved slowly, pumping his pelvis like the thorax of a wasp. He looked down at the place where their bodies joined, then at her face, then at his penis again. He felt the shaft tighten with arousal the more he thought about it. He was pounding Amelia, Amelia Ashton, and he was doing it outside on the grass.

Amelia clutched at the grass she was lying on, ripping up the blades with her hands as Louis increased the momentum. She wanted to scream out but didn't dare. Other wedding guests were walking by just feet away from where they writhed. Louis started to grunt. Amelia silenced him by putting her hand over his mouth.

'Careful,' she whispered. Louis took it as a cue to slow down. 'No,' Amelia hissed. 'Harder. But quieter.'

Louis complied straight away. Amelia continued to push upwards against him, kneading his buttocks beneath her hands. Pinching him. Goading him towards his climax. She could already feel herself at the edge of hers. The muscles of her vagina were tightening around him. Her stomach felt as though it was filling up with helium. She was growing increasingly dizzy, as though the excitement might make her pass out at any moment.

'Oh, Louis,' she called. She couldn't keep quiet this time. The sound of her calling his name told Louis that he too could stop holding on. He began to thrash about like a fish out of water almost straight away. He was throwing his head back as he made the last few gigantic thrusts. Shouting out without making a sound. His semen pouring into her body like a flood.

He couldn't stay silent anymore. Amelia dug her fingers into him and pressed her body against him to catch the full force. His penis seemed to have expanded to fill the whole of her body. Her orgasm seemed to be driving up through the centre of her spine and coming out through her mouth.

'Yes! Yes! Yes! That's wonderful.'

Her vagina gripped him like a possessive fist, trying to keep him inside her for all time. She had never had such a powerful orgasm out of doors.

Louis collapsed and rolled off her, leaving a trail of his semen on the lacy garter that circled her thigh. Louis squeezed her hand and tried to find the words . . . But he couldn't. Instead, they dissolved into laughter and lay side by side in the bushes for a while, watching the elegant feet of the other guests pass them by. It was as if they were children hiding from the grown-ups again.

Chapter Fourteen

'HELLO.'

When Amelia emerged from the loos, her lipstick back in place and her stockings finally discarded altogether, she said hello automatically to another familiar face. There were so many Lusardis at the wedding that she had given up trying to remember names, though most of them were called Louis or Louisa anyway. But the elegant man in the morning suit didn't quite have the brooding Lusardi look about him and this time Amelia couldn't resist trying to find out where she had met him before.

'Excuse me,' she tapped him shyly on the elbow. 'Are you Karis's uncle Gaetano by any chance?'

'No,' said the man with a distinctly English accent that betrayed no hint of Mafia at all. 'I'm a friend of the groom. Crispin Hardcastle. How do you do?' He extended his hand.

'How do you do?' said Amelia.

They looked at each other without saying

anything for a moment. Amelia racked her brains for another gambit to keep the conversation going. This man was gorgeous . . . and she was free. Louis had gone to drive his grandmother back to her hotel for the night.

'That's it!' said Amelia suddenly. 'Concorde. On Tuesday. We sat next to each other and you slept for the whole flight. I was very disappointed. I don't often get to sit next to someone I think I might like to talk to.'

Crispin scratched his chin. 'I'm sorry,' he said. 'I don't recall . . . I have a terrible memory for faces. Though I think I may have done myself a disservice by not remembering yours.'

Amelia blushed. It wasn't the first time that week she had been accused of being forgettable. 'I think I must look quite different when I've got my make-up on.'

'Yes,' said Crispin. 'Quite ravishing . . .' Then he almost blushed. 'Well,' he muttered awkwardly. 'I suppose I ought to get back to my table. I'm supposed to be looking after Tim's sister Caroline, you know.'

'Lucky girl,' Amelia breathed.

'I'll see you again before the day's over, no doubt.' Crispin started back in the direction of the marquee. He nodded uncertainly. 'Yes, I'll see you again.'

Suddenly Amelia doubted that she ever would see him again and reached out to stop him.

'I'm sure Caroline can spare you for a moment or two,' she said hurriedly. 'I don't know England all that well, being half-American. I noticed that there is quite a good view of the surrounding countryside from the front of the club and I wonder whether you might be so kind as to show me a few landmarks.'

'The landmarks?' Crispin was puzzled. 'I'm afraid that I wouldn't be much use to you there. I'm not actually from around here myself.'

'Oh well, perhaps you could tell me what kind of trees those are instead?' she said, pointing outside vaguely. Amelia wasn't taking no for an answer. She took Crispin by the arm and led him out onto the veranda. 'You look like a man who knows a thing or two about plants.'

She took his hand between her palms and stroked it as she looked deep into his eyes. The penny dropped.

'Plants? Ah yes, plants,' said Crispin.

The new Mrs Williamson was standing on the veranda with her husband, surrounded by a gaggle of girls all wanting to know about the dress and dying, of course, to see the ring. As Amelia passed, Karis caught her eye and smiled. When Tim caught Crispin's eye, his response was to open his mouth with the expression of a confused fish. Wasn't that his sister's man?

Amelia and Crispin walked further down the garden, to the point where the bright lights that shone from the clubhouse no longer cast any glow onto the grass. Now Crispin strode purposefully on. Amelia tripped behind him, happening unexpectedly upon an uneven path of crazy paving slabs.

'Where are we going?' she asked.

'You wanted to see some plants.'

The dying sun suddenly appeared from behind

the clouds and illuminated a large greenhouse which stood next to the perimeter fence. It was here that the golf-club gardener nurtured the beautiful flowers that grew in the borders and decorative urns outside the clubhouse as well as a few bits and bobs for his personal use. Crispin pushed the door open and motioned Amelia inside. The air in the greenhouse was hot and heavy with the musty scent of ripening tomatoes. A vine, hung with miniature bunches of hard, little green grapes, wound its way along struts suspended from the ceiling. A swelling melon hung suggestively from .a sling that was made from an old pair of tights.

'Tropical, isn't it?' said Crispin.

'Sort of,' Amelia replied. 'What a find!'

'Yes, I noticed it earlier on when I had to come outside for a smoke.'

Crispin closed the aluminium-edged door that sealed the greenhouse like a biosphere. The heat was stifling. Amelia felt her head grow light and wasn't sure whether her giddiness was caused by a lack of oxygen or the heady smell of Crispin's aftershave as he pulled her close to him and shuffled her backwards to lean against a compost bag.

'I think I remember meeting you on Concorde now,' he whispered hotly in her reddening ear. 'You gave me quite an erotic dream. When I woke up I was terrified that it might have been a wet one . . .'

A giddy thrill rocketed through Amelia's limbs.

'I would have noticed,' she told him as she reached out to finger his expensively silky tie.

145

'And I'm sure I would have persuaded you to give me your phone number . . .'

Suddenly Crispin lifted Amelia's long red hair from her shoulders and kissed her carefully at the nape of her neck. Then his lips moved from her neck to her mouth. His tongue, flickering against hers, tasted of champagne and wedding cake. She felt intoxicated just from tasting him. His hands, the hands she had dreamed of holding while dozing on the plane, held her like a piece of delicate eggshell porcelain. One supporting each of her narrow shoulder-blades.

'I hope you don't mind if I kiss you,' he added, after he had taken the liberty.

'I guess it's too late now,' she murmured into his mouth.

He smiled and leaned harder against her. Amelia's strappy high-heeled sandals slipped on the wet floor of the greenhouse and her legs parted further around his. Crispin continued to kiss her, letting his tongue play teasingly over her lips as his hips slowly began to grind against hers. She could feel his hardening penis through his pinstriped grey trousers and her more than slightly creased skirt.

Crispin's hands weren't quite so gentle now. They moved over her tender breasts with professional precision. Seeking out the nipples which poked through the thin silk of her blouse, he teased them to two hard peaks that almost ached from the friction of the material against them. Amelia was glad when he finally rolled the blouse out of the way and her tingling breasts were momentarily quietened by the caress of the

146

warm greenhouse air.

'You've got fantastic tits,' he commented. Amelia giggled at the sound of such coarse words in such a cultured accent and wrapped a hot leg snakily around his tailored thigh. Crispin took her left breast in his hand and squeezed it appreciatively, making Amelia throw back her head in delight. Then his head dipped to gently kiss a longing nipple. His tongue swirled around it before his lips sucked it in between sharp teeth.

'Oh,' Amelia gasped.

'Did that hurt?' he asked.

'No, no. Carry on.'

'My pleasure.' Crispin moved his attention to the other breast. Amelia cupped the back of his beautiful grey-streaked head and pulled him closer still. She felt for the moment as though all her sensation was gathered in her breasts. They tingled, almost hummed with pleasure as they swelled out to his touch. Oh, incredible, she murmured. She wondered if he could smell Louis on her skin. Then his teeth closed on a nipple in the gentlest of bites. Amelia cried out in joy and had to stop herself from screaming by biting on the back of her own hand.

Then his kiss began to drift downwards. She felt the butterfly path of his lips across her belly to the low slung waistband of her skirt. His hands closed around her waist as his tongue probed at her belly button. After seconds of this torture she was helping him to unbutton the delicate mother of pearl buttons at her hip until the tailored skirt slid soundlessly to the greenhouse floor.

She was wearing no knickers, since Louis had

discarded them somewhere further up the garden earlier on. Now Crispin's hands slid freely over her buttocks and when he lifted her up to sit on a plastic-covered compost bag on one of the shelves, the coolness of it made her shiver.

'Open your legs,' he instructed in a whisper, a warm strong hand on each of her thighs.

Amelia complied, sliding her legs apart until Crispin could move easily between them. He kissed her face tenderly, then he dropped to his knees on the floor before her. His hands glided slowly towards her crotch until his thumbs brushed with the slightest of touches against her labia.

'So beautiful,' he murmured.

'Oh, yes,' Amelia sighed, barely able to draw a shuddering breath. She felt him part her lips as if he were parting the petals of some rare flower. She was already wet, she knew it. Her thighs were damp with perspiration. She heard his breathing grow heavier. The sounds of the wedding party in the distance were faint now, drowned out by his breathing and her heart.

'Yes, yes,' she whispered as he moved so close to her that she could feel the warm air of his breathing flowing right into her. She looked down at the shadow of his head, wishing that she could see his pink tongue stretching out in the darkness to touch her in the place where she ached for him. The first contact made her draw in her breath. Her hands tightly gripped the edge of the splintery greenhouse shelf.

Crispin drew his tongue along the length of her vagina with a cruel slow relish. Amelia's fingers almost cracked with the strain of holding on to the shelf. She shuddered at the sensation of his warm, wet tongue against her wetter labia. He used his tongue as skilfully as any finger to flick at her hardening clitoris, sending spasms of pure ecstasy shooting up her spine. She was torn between needing to hang on to her precarious perch and wanting to grasp the back of his head again, to force him to penetrate deeper and deeper with his long, strong tongue.

'Crispin,' she murmured. He responded to his name with an extra hard lick. 'This feels so good.'

The flattery made him work even harder.

Amelia felt so happy, so hot. Condensation dripped from the ceiling onto her damp, naked thighs, making her laugh out loud. Crispin continued to lick at her dutifully, enjoying the rising pitch of her squeals and sighs. She couldn't help but clamp her thighs tightly around his burning hot ears. His fingers dug hard into her buttocks as the temperature in the greenhouse rose out of control . . .

'Crash!'

A well-aimed champagne bottle suddenly came flying through the greenhouse roof, landing just inches away. Amelia ducked back from the shattering glass. Crispin was protected by her fast-closing thighs. Amelia, luckily, was protected by the tomatoes.

'What the . . .'

Crispin was on his feet in seconds.

'Are you OK?'

Amelia nodded. She had nearly been more than

OK. Crispin wrenched open the greenhouse door and ran up the steps towards the clubhouse in search of the culprit. Amelia dragged on her compost-speckled skirt and followed him disconsolately, but at a respectable distance, up the crazy-paving path to the fast-fading party.

She wondered if cousin Caroline was throwing a wobbly over the loss of the party's most eligible man.

Oh well, Amelia sighed. She guessed that she had had her share. Amelia glanced at her watch. It was Saturday night. It was almost half past ten. She suddenly remembered that she had a rendezvous to keep at a certain bar.

Chapter Fifteen

AMELIA DROVE LIKE a demon back to London but when she arrived at the bar, just two minutes late, Sue already looked agitated. She began to put on her jacket and got up from her seat even as Amelia walked towards her. Before Amelia had time to buy a drink, Sue slipped a crumpled piece of paper into her hand.

'Seems like you put in a couple of extra hours last night,' Sue said sarcastically.

'You found your phone?' Amelia asked.

'Yes, thank you. I found my phone. Looks like I've become your answering service though. Your Hampstead job wants to see you again. Tonight. As soon as possible. That's the address.'

Great. A score. Amelia's heart-rate soared. She looked at the address on the scrap torn from Sue's diary.

'But that's Wales,' she said incredulously.

'That's right,' Sue replied.

Amelia had expected him to be in London. 'What's he doing out there?'

'It's his country retreat, I guess,' Sue explained. 'Can you do it, Natalie? I'd like to help you out but I've got an old friend coming into town on Sunday and I can't afford to upset him, if you know what I mean. Mr Hampstead says he'll pay for a hire car or petrol and all other expenses. Have a nice drive, babe.' With that, Sue kissed her on the cheek and almost ran to the door where a taxi was already waiting to take her to her rendezvous. The barman, who was beginning to recognise blonde-wigged Amelia and to know her order, placed a vodka and tonic in front of her.

Amelia looked at the address in her hand one more time. Wales? That was miles away. It would take her hours to get there and she was meant to be back in the States by Sunday night. Of course she couldn't do this job. She just didn't have the time. But, on the other hand, she reasoned, this could be the last opportunity she would have to get to know her hero. She had already forgotten the address in Hampstead and even if she could remember it, she could hardly send a letter.

Making her mind up as suddenly as she had decided to do the very first job, Amelia pushed the vodka and tonic back towards the barman.

'Thanks,' she told him, 'but I had better not have that – I'm driving tonight.'

Four hours later, Amelia looked from the sign on the gatepost to the scrap of paper in her hand and back again in dismay. Both read 'Ty Ysgol' and she had followed the directions she had been given to the letter but the tall, glowering house which stood in front of her now was nothing but a crumbling shell. Half the windows didn't even seem to have any glass in them, let alone a light.

Amelia inched the little red hire car through the gateposts and closer to the door with the intention of avoiding as much of the mud as she possibly could. However, while swerving to avoid a particularly boggy patch, she managed to get herself completely stuck. The wheels began to spin frantically, sending jets of mud up behind her. It was no use whirring the engine, that would only get her in deeper still. Amelia looked at the quagmire which still remained between her and the house and then gazed woefully at her elegant leather pumps. She hadn't thought to bring walking boots.

She was stuck. For once in her life she had no mobile phone about her person and even if she had one she would probably have found that there was no reception in this God-forsaken place. There was no way she would be able to get the car out of the ditch by herself and as darkness crept further in and no lights in the house went on, it appeared that there was no one in Ty Ysgol either. Amelia felt like crying. What she wouldn't have given to be in a nice warm hotel suite now. She switched off the engine and turned off the lights. No point in running the battery down. She tapped her fingers on the steering wheel.

What choice did she have but to get inside that horrible house and try to light a fire before it was completely pitch dark?

Amelia took a deep breath and opened the car door. She pondered taking her shoes off for a moment but decided that the feel of that mud through her stockings would be worse than ruining a pair of Manolo Blahniks. She swung her legs out through the car-door with the grace of a supermodel and swore like a fishwife when her shoes hit the shit.

Ten feet had never seemed so far.

The splintered wooden door of the house continued to creak on its hinges for minutes after Amelia had opened it. She found her way into the kitchen and stood on a floor of cold worn flagstones, looking in disgust at her mud-caked feet. She could barely see her shoes – two hundred pounds worth of baby soft suede – but she managed a sorry smile when she thought how much Rowena would laugh to see her superstar now, breaking the legs off a chair to light a fire . . . and if Rowena had known how Amelia came to be in such a sorry position in the middle of nowhere, she would have roared with hysterics.

An old newspaper served as a firelighter and pretty soon the room was filled with the glow of a feeble flame and a considerable amount of smoke. The chimney was blocked too, no doubt. Amelia threw her ruined shoes on the floor in a moment of extreme fury, kicked one into the grate, then swiftly pulled it out again before it got burned.

'I'm sorry, I'm sorry, I'm sorry!' she screamed at no one in particular. 'Could I wake up now please?'

But it wasn't a dream.

It was almost a nightmare.

She checked her watch in the pathetic glow of the flame. There were hours and hours till dawn.

Gingerly she picked up an old sack that was lying in the corner, checked it for rats, and, finding none, made herself a little nest by the fire. She hugged her knees tightly in an attempt to get warmer and felt very sorry for herself indeed.

Suddenly the smoke swirled backwards from the fire and Amelia was aware that somewhere behind her a door had been opened. She turned cautiously, making sure that she had picked up a fire poker first. She heard a step behind her on the hard stone floor, heavy breathing, then a familiar cough.

'Warm enough for you?' Tony Devonfield asked.

Amelia whirled around, brandishing the rusty poker. She had been waiting in this God-forsaken hole for what seemed like nearly three hours and had had plenty of time to come to the conclusion that the customer is not always right.

'Thank God you're here,' she snorted. 'I hope you've got a Land Rover or something. My car is completely jammed in the mud and all I want to do is get it out and go home.'

Tony Devonfield was laughing.

'It's not funny,' Amelia continued. 'I'm not staying here a moment longer than I have to and you owe me two hundred pounds for a pair of ruined shoes.'

'Why? Because you can't follow instructions?'

'What do you mean?'

Amelia was standing up now, clutching her thin jacket around her for its pathetic amount of warmth.

'Well,' he explained, 'if you had followed my

instructions you would have arrived not at the house but at the barn, which is where I live. I assumed that you had decided not to come at all, but then I noticed that the chimney was on fire.'

'On fire!'

'An exaggeration perhaps.' Devonfield had moved across the room and was already putting out the puny imitation of a conflagration that Amelia had started. 'I'll just make this safe and then we'll go across to the barn. If you don't want to stay, you don't have to. But I don't think your car will be moving until tomorrow.'

'You can take me to the nearest train station and arrange to have that crappy hatchback sent on.'

'I'd like to but I don't have a car,' said Devonfield with a wry smile. Amelia took her head in her hands. Of course he didn't. He was a bloody hermit. 'And much as I'd love to walk you back to the nearest village, I'm afraid that I have a bad foot.'

'I can't believe it.'

'You'll have to stay here until the morning.'

Amelia resigned herself to her fate. Bad-temperedly.

Devonfield finished putting out the fire and led Amelia out of the room. There was no light but the feeble beam of his torch and so she had little choice but to take his hand in order to negotiate the unfamiliar territory. He told her the story of the house. That he had bought it just under a year ago and had intended to do it up but, after converting the barn, he found that he had lost his steam. That he was becoming too involved in

156

'other projects' to get on with the DIY. Amelia longed to press him for details on the other projects but decided instead to bite her tongue.

They reached the back door of the house which led onto a mud-filled yard. The barn was still a long way off, hidden by a wall around the house. Amelia looked in desperation at the moonlit mud before her and then at her feet, now clad only in torn stockings. Without saying a word, Devonfield scooped her up in his arms and carried her across. Amelia was taken aback by his strength and noticed, of course, that despite his 'bad foot', he had no sign of a limp. She wanted to scream at him. But something in her resolve to get back to London had already melted. She wanted desperately to see the barn. To see the home of her hero.

Devonfield opened the door to the barn with a flourish. The warmth hit them immediately.

'Sit down by the fire,' he instructed. 'And take your stockings off. They look soaked.'

Amelia gladly did as she was told.

As Devonfield disappeared into another room, she looked around the comfortable kitchen and reflected on the bizarre nature of her position. A country kitchen in Wales. Hardly the kind of establishment you expect to visit as a hooker. But then, she considered, she was hardly the kind of girl you expect to be a hooker. While she was thinking, Devonfield re-entered the kitchen carrying two brandy glasses filled with swirling amber liquid.

'Here, to warm you up and calm your temper.'

Amelia took the glass with a smile. She sipped

hesitantly at the brandy. It wasn't her favourite drink but a couple of years of dining in the world's finest restaurants enabled her to tell at once that it was expensive stuff. She appreciated that.

'Nice place you have here,' she said.

'Thanks. It suits me . . . Have you eaten?' he asked.

'No,' Amelia replied.

'I've been cooking all afternoon.'

Now this was bizarre.

'Cooking?'

'I bake my own bread. The shop in the village isn't much cop on a Bank Holiday. But then I suppose you don't move to this part of the country for the conveniences of life.'

'Why do you come here at all?' Amelia couldn't help asking. 'Your place in London is so nice . . .'

'It's not my place, unfortunately. I was house-sitting for a friend.'

'Oh.' Amelia felt strangely pleased. No wonder she had been unable to find a photo of him over the fireplace. She took a good look at the kitchen. No particularly feminine touches there. 'So, you live here all the time?'

'That's right.'

'On your own.'

'That's right.'

'You must get lonely.'

'Not really. I don't like people very much,' he replied.

'Oh.' Amelia shivered.

Devonfield tried to smile.

He really had been cooking all day. Not just bread but a wonderful casserole which, to Amelia, tasted all the better for the long drive from London and her cold hungry wait in the house. He brought out wine to go with it. Expensive wine that made Amelia glow inside. They chatted about lots of things. The countryside. The weather. But each time Amelia thought she might guide him onto the subject of his music, Devonfield changed the subject and pretended not to hear her, or went to fill her glass.

'We've been talking all night. I feel like I must have bored you rigid,' he said suddenly, starting to get up.

'No, no.' Amelia automatically reached out and touched his arm. Devonfield stopped on his path from the table to the sink and looked at her. Amelia's heart fluttered in her mouth. She was sure that she saw something other than lust in his gaze. 'No, I'm not bored at all.'

Devonfield swallowed hard.

'You don't have to say that.'

Amelia piled up some plates and carried them to the draining board. When she had put them down, she remained beside him, waiting for him to suggest the next move.

'Shall we wash up?' she asked. 'Or shall we go to bed.'

Chapter Sixteen

'THE BATHROOM'S THROUGH there,' he waved in the direction of the end of the hall. 'It would be nice if you could pin your hair up,' he added shyly. Amelia padded down the hallway with her bag in her hand. The heat from the kitchen hadn't reached that far. She pushed open the door and stepped gingerly onto the cold lino. To her relief, there was no tutu hanging from the shower rail this time, just plump towels and an unexpected vase of dried flowers.

Amelia touched up her make-up quickly. She was anxious to be back in the warm, but also anxious to be back with Devonfield, as if two minutes away from him would start to decay the bridge she felt she had been making towards him. She pinned her hair up in an untidy top-knot and sprayed Chanel No. 5 across her throat as though she was preparing herself to meet a lover.

When she had finished, she went in search of him. He wasn't in the kitchen any more. Amelia followed the gentle strains of a solo cello until she found the bedroom. Devonfield was in the corner of the room, lighting up a candelabrum which stood on an old wooden trunk. Amelia sighed audibly. He turned around and greeted her with a nervous smile.

'I hope you won't be too cold,' he said. 'I haven't got round to putting in any central heating yet . . .'

Amelia sat down on the edge of the bed and shrugged. 'And I'm afraid I don't have any spare stockings,' she explained.

'That's OK.' Devonfield was already beside her. Kissing her exposed neck, then just breathing in the scent of her. He slid an arm across her shoulders. Amelia closed her eyes and relaxed into his arms. She lay back on the clean white sheets and dreamed as he began to unfasten her dress.

Beneath the soft grey jersey of her dress, she was wearing a stiff, satin basque. The boning followed her own curves perfectly. It fitted tightly to her narrow waist, making her look like the eternal hourglass of every fantasy. Of his fantasy.

Amelia touched the buttons of his shirt and began to unfasten them one by one. She slid her hands beneath the cotton and across his hard, wide shoulders. Devonfield shrugged the shirt off. Amelia responded by freeing her arms from their jersey confines. Devonfield unbuttoned his soft, worn jeans and soon there was nothing between them but her basque and a pair of silky shorts.

Amelia traced her fingers over the square edge of Devonfield's jaw, then she ran them through his hair, so thick and soft in her hands. With his locks still twisted in her fingers she tugged him gently down towards her again and kissed his nervously smiling mouth.

She felt him shift his weight carefully onto her reclining body. His legs were either side of her now. His groin pressed urgently against the burning hot triangle of desire at the top of her legs. Amelia grasped his firm, silk-covered buttocks in her longing hands and used them to pull him closer still. Moaning softly, she ground her pelvis upwards against his.

'Natalie,' Devonfield whispered. The word made her tense up before she remembered that, to him, Natalie was her name. She relaxed again and brushed her hand tenderly along his back. Through the silk of his boxer shorts she could feel the hardness of his swelling dick pressing into her as the touch of her hands aroused him further. Breathing harder, she squeezed her hand in between their rocking bodies and began to ease the waistband of the boxers down. He raised himself up on his arms to give her more room and soon his pulsing shaft was swaying free in the air between them. Then he lay back down between her thighs and ran his hands over her hips in their complicated casing of lace and satin. His fingers hovered hesitantly at the scalloped lace edge of her lacy little knickers.

Amelia held her breath for what seemed like an eternity until he finally began to edge the knickers slowly down her legs, rolling himself over onto the bed beside her as he did so. Amelia raised her hips to the ceiling to help him ease them free from her buttocks. Then she rolled over and waited in silence as he unfastened the hooks at the back of the basque one by one. When all were undone, Amelia turned and lay on her back again, naked before his gaze. Her body was half hidden in his shadow, half golden in the flickering light of the candles.

She heard him gasp as he saw the smooth lines of her body in the half-light. He ran a hand slowly up her hip to her waist like a sculptor appraising a goddess hewn from stone. A cool breeze drifting in from the window made her shiver. Devonfield climbed on top of her again, only partly to shield her from the cold. He raised himself from her body ever so slightly and delicately traced a path up the inside of her thigh with trembling fingers. Amelia sighed and responded by wrapping her own fingers around his aching shaft.

His smooth penis felt so warm in her hand. It was pulsing, longing to be inside her. She brought her fingers back up to her mouth, licked them for lubrication, and began to slick his foreskin back and forth with long, deliciously slow strokes. Devonfield drew deep breaths sharply and grasped Amelia's thigh so tightly that she felt sure he must have left fingermarks. Then he touched his fingers to her vagina, hesitantly, making her shudder with desire. Carefully he parted her labia and dipped one finger inside.

'That's nice,' Amelia murmured.

He moved the finger in and out, keeping in time with her hand on his shaft.

Amelia could almost hear the beating of her heart in the nervous silence of the room.

Impulsively she let go of Devonfield's penis and clasped him against her in a lover's embrace, feeling the warm caress of his shaft against her soft inner thigh. It nudged so gently yet insistently against her labia and begged to be allowed inside.

Suddenly, Devonfield broke away from her and reached over to the chest of drawers which stood beside the bed. Seconds later he had a condom in his hand and was rolling it over his penis while Amelia caressed his balls with one hand and her own labia with the other. When he was ready, they looked at each other for a final, tense moment as a flicker of uncertainty passed across his steel grey eyes, in which there mingled passion and fear of their still being hardly more than strangers to each other.

'Are you sure?' Devonfield asked.

Amelia nodded.

Devonfield lunged forward and into her, his breath escaping him in a low grunt. Amelia called out in the darkness, her limbs suddenly flooded with the sensation of the union that she seemed to have been anticipating for so long. Devonfield lay still, as if the first thrust had taken all his energy. Amelia wrapped her legs around his back and rocked so that he was deeper still. They lay like that, locked together, for mere moments, but the tension between them stretched the minutes into hours. Amelia felt hypersensitive. His chestnut head was buried in her shoulder. She could smell the fresh, clean scent of his shampoo, mingled with the salty tang of sweat upon his skin. The skin on his back was smoother than a wave-worn pebble beneath her fingers.

'Tony,' she murmured. 'Tony.' Trying the name out for size as it rolled off her tongue.

As if her words had awoken him from some kind of spell, he began to move again now, gently rocking up and down, withdrawing from her body then slipping back into her inch by delicious inch. They seemed to fit together so perfectly. The movement between them was so natural, it was as if they had been together for years instead of mere hours. Devonfield raised himself above her, locking his arms into position. Amelia gazed down into the space between them but could only imagine what they must look like where they joined, coming together and apart in the flickering candlelight.

Devonfield moved so carefully. First a thrust to the left, then to the right. He wanted to stimulate every part of her welcoming passage. Amelia let out an involuntary squeal as she felt the domed head of his shaft touch the front wall of her vagina. She gripped his buttocks until her fingers left white marks as the gentle nudging inside her sent pins and needles shooting along her spine.

Then he collapsed down onto her again. His thrusting was becoming more insistent, as if he could no longer bear to take things at such an agonisingly slow pace. Amelia flung an arm around his neck. With the other she enwrapped his back. He was moving so fast now that she could barely keep up with him. His breath in her ear became one long ecstatic groan.

Desperately Amelia pushed her body upwards against his, forcing contact along every hot inch of their rapt and shaking bodies. She wanted to feel his shaft grate against her clitoris each time he withdrew, like a bow drawing notes from a violin. Now her legs were quaking and she could barely control her movements except to push up and up and up.

Suddenly, Devonfield's body grew rigid. His head was thrown backwards as he cried to the creaking beams in the ceiling above their heads. Amelia responded to his call with a final skyward thrust of her buttocks. They were locked together, pumping into one another. Amelia felt giddy with sensation, her hands hard on his buttocks, pressing down, harder, harder, making the contact complete.

They rolled apart and lay panting side by side on the cool white sheets. Amelia stretched her arm back lazily and reached for the antique bedstead. Devonfield grasped the elegant hand that was in the air and brought it to his mouth for a kiss.

Chapter Seventeen

AMELIA DREW A deep breath. Devonfield's own breathing had settled back into a normal pattern now and he seemed to be relaxed. She had to find out more about him before it was time to leave but, strangely, the first question which burned in her mind was to ask him what she was doing there.

'So,' she rolled onto her side and whispered into his ear. 'Why do you sleep with prostitutes?'

She thought that she could almost hear a smile form on his handsome face but he said nothing.

'I mean,' Amelia continued, 'it's not as if you're horribly deformed, or nasty or even perverted. I could think of a dozen girls who would sleep with you for nothing . . .' Devonfield placed a finger across her moving lips.

'Do you want to know why or are you going to answer the question for me?'

'I'm sorry . . . I was chattering on . . .' Her voice trailed away and Amelia bit her lip as she waited nervously for the answer.

Devonfield inhaled noisily. 'Natalie . . . I sleep with prostitutes because I don't trust anybody.'

'Why not?'

'It's a complicated story,' he began. 'I don't want to bore you.'

'Bore me,' she murmured.

'OK,' he sighed. 'A very long time ago, probably before you were even old enough to know what sex is, I was in the rather fortunate position of being quite a big name in the record industry.'

'Oh really?' Amelia pretended ignorance.

'Yeah. I played with a band who had a bit of success. Sold a few records. Made a bit of money.'

What an understatement that was! thought Amelia. Devonfield's band had had seven number ones.

'And I got all the trappings which go with that kind of success. Lots of "friends". Lots of "lovers",' he continued. 'But then I got tired of the whole scene and decided to drop out. I wanted to do something different, something experimental. I pulled out of the band halfway through a world tour and never went back.

'It was then that I quickly discovered that the people who would have "done anything" for me before the split felt that I had let them down and detached themselves from me like glutted leeches falling off a drained cow. Talk about fair-weather friends. It's taken me a long time to get over that. The fact that people who had seemed to be so close to me really cared so very little. I've been too cynical to trust anyone since.'

'Women in particular, eh?'

Devonfield sighed. 'At least when I pay a girl, I know exactly why she's here. Though,' he added in a whisper, 'I'd rather you were here of your own accord.'

Amelia sat up in bed and moved across him so that she looked down into his face, obscured though it was by darkness. She didn't say another word but gently kissed his frowning mouth.

Chapter Eighteen

THAT WHISPERED CONVERSATION in the middle of the night had seemed like a breakthrough but the next morning Amelia awoke to find herself alone. The pillow beside her still bore the vague indent to show where his head had lain, but Devonfield was long gone.

As she tidied up her hair at the dressing table, she noticed an envelope. She almost didn't open it, forgetting for a moment that as far as Devonfield was concerned, Natalie was her name. When she did, her heart dropped like a stone. The envelope was stuffed with twenty crisp fifty-pound notes and a small hand-written message, telling her that he had gone out for a walk and would be most grateful to find that she had gone by the time he returned. Her car was no longer stuck in the mud, the note continued. The men from the local garage had come with a tow-truck at dawn.

Amelia gathered her clothes together in a blur, trying to fight back the inexplicable tears which were gathering behind her sleepy eyes. What had she expected? she asked herself. She might have warmed to him, but as far as he was concerned, Amelia was just a hooker. At best he would think that she was only interested in him for the money and at worst he would be looking down on her, thinking her not just a hooker but a sucker, falling for a client, a man who bought girls like she bought shoes.

Amelia wandered barefoot towards the door, slowly, praying that she could bump into him in the act of leaving. She would blurt out her story, say that she got involved with the whole business because she was desperate to work with him, not for him. It was almost a true story, after all.

But when she looked out of the kitchen window, Amelia saw that Devonfield was halfway up the hill and heading in the opposite direction to the barn. He wouldn't be back for hours. He really didn't want to see her.

She made herself a coffee and tried to pull herself together. It was then that it struck her, the fact that he was so far away could be a blessing in disguise.

Amelia recalled that Devonfield had said that the barn was not only the place where he lived, but the place where he worked. What was he working on? It had to be new music and that new music had to be somewhere in that barn. Amelia laid her coat down on the kitchen table and resolved that she had nothing to lose from exploring the barn now. She walked the length of the building, opening the unfamiliar doors until she came to one tiny door that was hiding a

171

narrow staircase. Feeling like a character from a fairy-tale about to stumble upon a monster, she crept up the little flight. At the top, the stairs turned a corner and there was another door. She rattled the handle. It was locked shut. Amelia thanked her mother for an expensive education and hatpins.

Pretty soon, she had the door open and found exactly what she had been looking for.

No wonder Devonfield had forgotten about bothering with the house when he had finished renovating the barn. Here in the roof he had the most amazing studio Amelia had ever seen. She wandered through the airy room, trailing her fingers along the huge mixing desk and the state-of-the-art keyboards that could have turned even the hopeless keyboard player from Amelia's touring band into Mozart.

She played a couple of experimental chords on the white baby grand which dominated the studio. With a toy like that, she would never bother to go into town either. Amelia couldn't resist bashing out a medley of her favourite tunes. As she was just about to launch into a forte version of 'New York, New York', she came to an abrupt halt. What was she doing? The sound of her playing had probably carried all the way to Cardiff!

In the silence after the last chord faded, she felt sure that she heard the door creak open. She stayed perfectly still, like a rabbit hiding from a hawk. There was no more noise. She breathed out again. She was still alone.

The studio was lit by a skylight. Amelia looked

out of it and saw to her horror that Devonfield had turned round and was heading back down the hill towards the house. The time she thought she had was suddenly cut in two. Luckily, Amelia knew exactly where to look next. She flew to the DAT player and lifted one of the tapes that was lying beside it. 'Opus Four' was scribbled on the label. No time to play it. Amelia would just have to hope that it wasn't a blank. Pocketing the tape, she raced back down the stairs, slamming the door behind her. She was in the car and out of the village before Devonfield made it back to the house.

Seeing her car pulling out into the road, Devonfield stopped walking back to the house and watched her. He was too far away to wave.

Chapter Nineteen

BACK IN LONDON, Amelia hunted out her DAT player before she even bothered to take off her filthy stockings.

Devonfield hadn't lost his touch. The music on the tape was every bit as good as the best tracks on 'Messages at Midnight'.

No, it was better.

Amelia sat on the edge of her chair as she listened to half an hour of the most exciting music she had ever heard. There were no lyrics, but she could already feel those forming in her head. This was the real thing.

She rewound the tape and slipped it into her pocket, glowing with delight at her discovery. Now that she had listened to it, she could attend to business. The answer-machine flashed angrily. Three newspapers waited unread on her door-mat. She picked up the top one and smiled. 'Tracey Gostello in Big Baby shock.' He looked pissed off. Understandably.

Amelia wondered whether she would ever get

paid for the session she had done with him.

The answer-machine tape was full. Rowena, furious. Rowena, furious. Rowena, furious. Amelia's flight back to New York would be leaving in less than two hours. Where was she? Amelia called straight away to put Rowena's mind at rest and dutifully promised that, come hell or high water, she would be on the next flight out of town.

As it was, Amelia made it to the airport by the skin of her teeth. She had no time whatsoever to enjoy the luxury of the first-class passengers' lounge that day. She was rushed straight onto the plane from passport control by two stewardesses out of prison warden school. As she scuttled down the walkway, she could hear the airport announcer putting out a final call for passenger Ashton and couldn't suppress a blush.

Unfortunately, the hostess explained as she relieved Amelia of her coat and handed her a couple of newspapers, due to her late arrival, they were unable to give Amelia the seat she had requested. She wouldn't be next to the window after all.

'No problem,' Amelia assured her, eager not to create any more fuss. 'I'm so knackered that I think I could sit on the wings and still be happy.'

The hostess indicated Amelia's seat with a wave of her hand. Amelia reached up to put her handbag in the overhead locker, then she looked at the man who would be in the seat next to her and froze. She started to fetch the bag down again and backed out into the aisle.

Perhaps the wing would be a better option.

'I can't sit there,' she hissed to the hostess.

The man in the window-seat was snoring lightly. Amelia had completely forgotten that she wasn't the only major recording star to be flying back to New York that day. It didn't seem awfully sensible to stick around until Tracey Gostello woke up and ask him whether he had got himself a new chauffeur yet.

'Are there any other seats?' Amelia asked.

'Not in first class, madam,' the hostess replied.

So Amelia flew back to New York in standard but when she arrived at JFK with cramp in her knees she decided that it had been a small price to pay. She tapped the DAT in her pocket. The next time she made that flight it would be in her own private Learjet.

Rowena met her at the airport.

'My god, Amelia, I have been working overtime to defend your honour this last week,' she complained. 'First the model and then Gostello. How could you? He was furious. Simply furious. He said that he refused to record for Midnight ever again unless the label dropped you first.'

'Am I dropped?' Amelia asked, almost disinterested.

'No.' A broad grin spread across Rowena's face. 'Gostello's blood belongs to Midnight. He couldn't leave us if he tried. But I'm afraid you won't be credited on his new album, of course.'

'Oh dear.' Amelia was almost glad.

A limousine was waiting by the terminal doors. Frankie was sitting in the front next to the chauffeur. As Amelia approached, he waved hello to his wayward charge but didn't manage to raise a smile.

'He feels guilty,' Rowena explained in a whisper, which was pointless since, as usual, Frankie was listening to Whitesnake on his Discman. 'Thinks he should have kept a closer eye on you. Stopped you from giving us the slip. He cried to keep his job, you know. I hope that makes you feel bad.'

'I do, Rowena. I really do.'

The limo sped into New York. Amelia gazed out of the tinted windows, knowing that the outside world couldn't gaze in. Nothing had changed. As the buildings began to get taller, the streets were totally in shadow and the light was pushed further and further away. Amelia remembered the view from Devonfield's window. The Welsh hills that seemed to roll off endlessly into the distance. The green of the grass and the white and blue of the sky. Devonfield's brown back against the pure white sheets.

As she reached into her pocket for a tissue, Amelia felt the hard edge of the DAT case which still nestled there.

'So, what did you do in London?' Rowena asked gaily.

'I, er . . .' Amelia almost mentioned the tape. But then she said, 'This and that. I mostly just shopped.'

Chapter Twenty

ROWENA TURNED OFF her mobile phone with a smile.

'That was Frankenstein,' she said. 'He tells me that there's someone to see you down in the lobby.'

Amelia's heart leapt into her mouth then fell back down to where it should be again. What was the point in getting excited? It wasn't going to be him, was it? Not Devonfield.

Rowena was gathering her papers together. Blowing on Amelia's most recent signature to make sure that it didn't smudge. 'He's just passing through New York, apparently. I'll leave you alone, of course,' she was saying. 'After the way you dragged this guy through the papers, I don't particularly want to be within range when the shit starts to fly . . . Or when you start to kiss and make up for that matter.'

'It's not Gostello, is it?' Amelia pleaded. But Rowena was already opening the door. 'Rowena, you better not be sending Gostello up here unless you send me a lawyer up with him. I mean it. I'll sue you too . . .'

'Bye, Amelia.' Rowena slammed the door. And moments later there was another knock.

Amelia took a quick glance at her reflection in the mirror followed by a long, deep breath. She was in trouble now. How was she going to explain herself? 'Look, Tracey, I'm sorry. It's just that I was so bitter at not being able to get my chance of satisfaction with the man who invented the word? I'll take out an ad in *The Times* to say that the nappies were my idea?'

The knock came again. Less patient this time.

Amelia was still practising her lines. 'And your chauffeur was a terrible shag anyway. Will it be OK if I just write you a cheque for a six-figure sum right now?'

'Amelia, are you in there?'

Amelia recognised the Italian accent almost immediately. Thank heavens Gostello wasn't the only man she had dragged through the papers that month.

'Guido!' she opened the door to him with a smile made almost hysterical by relief. 'How lovely to see you! Come on in. How have you been? Well? Busy?' The guilt was already rising again. As he swaggered into the room, Guido had a slightly sniffy look on his face which suggested that she hadn't escaped the grovelling altogether that night.

'I am OK,' he said. He sat down on the blue chaise-longue that Amelia had once occupied with so much power and put his dirty big boots on the cushions. 'I 'ave been waiting for you to come back.'

'Oh, how lovely,' Amelia muttered.

He was wearing new jeans, without the embellishment of holes and motorbike grease. His tatty denim jacket had been replaced by a neat Schott leather bomber with fur around the collar.

'Nice jacket,' said Amelia as she automatically fetched the vodka and tonic.

'Hmm,' said Guido, wrinkling up his nose. 'It's OK, I s'pose. But after the case I'll be able to get something really good like Versace or D & G . . .'

The case? A chill ran down Amelia's back as she stood in front of the reclining Adonis, a full tumbler in each hand. The ice rattled against the glass as her hands shook.

'The case?' she said in a whisper.

'Yes, the case,' repeated Guido. 'My attorney, he say he thinks that two million isn't unreasonable in the light of the embarrassment that I 'ave suffered and the subsequent loss of earnings.' He stumbled over some of the words. He had obviously learned his legal position parrot-fashion.

'Two million?'

'Dollars.'

'Dollars?'

'The defendant can afford it,' said Guido flatly. He reached out and took one of the shaking glasses off Amelia's hands. 'Thank you,' he smiled as he took a small sip, 'but I like mine with a little more tonic.'

Amelia sank down onto the sofa opposite Guido and stared at him ashen-faced. Guido sipped at his drink but kept his eyes firmly on her too. They were head to head. It was like a shoot-out. He could hardly keep himself from breaking into a grin.

Finally Amelia cleared her throat. 'Have you spoken to Rowena about this?' she asked. 'I mean, there has to be another way. Think of the time it could take to drag this through the courts. And there's the chance that you might not even win. The defendant may have access to the very best lawyers in the land,' she added darkly.

Guido smoothed his hair back from his face with a smile.

'Indeed I'm sure that. Sayer and Rubenstein do . . .'

Amelia blinked.

'Sayer and Rubenstein?'

What did they have to do with this?

'You mean the advertising agency?'

'Yes.' Guido looked mildly shocked that she hadn't known who he was referring to all along. 'They used one of those pictures of me. The ones that the maid took when you left me tied to the bed.'

Amelia put her cool hands to her burning cheeks and exhaled with giddy relief.

'Sayer and Rubenstein,' she murmured again.

'They used a picture of me, with no clothes on, to advertise some underpants. I was twenty feet high over Times Square the morning after you left for London – with a sign saying 'Bet he wishes he was wearing his Kelvins'!

Amelia suddenly dissolved into laughter. 'Kelvins!' she squealed. 'Kelvins?'

'Exactly,' said Guido. 'As if I would put those

synthetics next to these balls. My career has been ruined. My agency gets forty calls a day from underpants manufacturers asking if I'll wear their boxers instead. I was invited to be on the panel at the Oprah Winfrey Show!'

'Oh, I'm so sorry,' Amelia spluttered between giggles.

Guido shot her a stern look.

'But you have to see that it is slightly funny,' she continued a little more softly. 'Oprah's a great show. And work's work, Guido,' she added. 'Before those pictures you were getting no calls at all.'

'I was working . . .'

'On and off.'

'I s'pose you're right,' Guido admitted grudgingly. 'And I 'ave agreed to do the Paulo de Angelo shoot.'

With that, he got to his feet and dropped his trousers.

He was already wearing the shoot props.

Amelia covered her mouth with her hands as she read the legend woven with black thread into the waistband of the simple, plain white shorts. 'Guido Agnelli at Paulo de Angelo'. They didn't look all that much different from Kelvins to her. Guido struck a pose for maximum effect.

'Very nice,' Amelia murmured appreciatively. 'Not even I have knickers that personalised.'

'You can borrow them if you like,' said Guido.

'Mmm, I might just take you up on that.' Amelia smiled and rose from her seat on the sofa to stand in front of him. She gazed admiringly at the long brown legs which descended from the soft white cotton and stroked a finger along his tight left thigh. 'But you'll have to take them off first.'

'My pleasure.'

Guido grinned and shook the Schott jacket off his shoulders so that it dropped heavily to the floor behind him. Amelia ran an admiring hand across his broad chest, warm beneath a clean grey T-shirt.

'But this time,' Guido warned her, 'you should remember that I now 'ave a lawyer.'

'Of course.' Amelia let her hands wander down the sides of Guido's waist until she reached the waistband of his personalised pants. She tucked just the tips of her fingers beneath the elastic and circled his waist, causing him to arch his back in pleasure and draw in a sharp breath at the coldness of her touch. She began to edge the white shorts down over his hips before she remembered that there would be no getting past those workman-like boots of his.

'Sit down again,' she instructed him softly.

Guido edged back until his bum touched the edge of the chaise-longue, careful not to trip over his jeans as he did so. Amelia sank slowly to her knees in front of him and searched for the thick laces of his boots beneath the wrinkled up denim. She undid the loose bows with a single tug and eased his feet free. He was wearing chunky, woollen socks that looked hand-knitted. Amelia pulled them off quickly and discarded them near his boots.

'Let's go into the bedroom,' she murmured.

'Am I allowed a last request?'

183

'Ha, ha.' Amelia took Guido by the hand and led him quickly to the bed. They stood side by side at the very foot of it, kissing gently. Then Amelia helped Guido strip off his T-shirt and he unbuttoned her blouse.

'Show me how you're going to pose,' she asked him.

Guido stepped away from her and flexed his pecs.

'Lovely,' Amelia murmured. 'That's really, really nice.'

Guido had pulled her close to him again. He slipped her blouse off her shoulders and cast it aside. He continued to kiss her as he unbuttoned her jeans and edged them down over her thighs. Amelia sat on the edge of the bed as he pulled them off over her feet. Then he held one foot in his hand and began to kiss that, little toe first. Amelia giggled and shuddered. She was ticklish. She had almost forgotten that.

Amelia lay back on the bed and closed her eyes as Guido started to kiss a path all the way up her leg. From her ankle to her knee was bearable, almost a welcome relief after the incredible sensitivity of her soft narrow feet, but from her knees up . . .

Amelia twisted handfuls of crisp cotton sheet in her fists as Guido lingered halfway up her inner thigh. Guido breathed her in, the musky-warm smell of her skin. He placed a long kiss on her thigh again, his lips pressed hard to her yielding flesh. Amelia sighed and let go of the sheets for long enough to reach out and touch his hair.

'Kiss me again,' she asked him softly, as if she

184

was afraid that if he stayed at her feet any longer she might peak way too soon.

Guido pulled himself up the bed until he lay on top of her. Amelia let her legs open around him and wrapped her arms around his back like a hydra. Guido ran his strong palms up the sides of her body, stopping when he came to the peachy silk of her bra. Amelia arched her back so that he could slip his hands beneath her and twist open the catch. He pushed the straps down over her arms and moments later they were both naked except for their pants.

'Still want to swap?' Amelia asked mischievously.

Guido raised himself away from her body and looked down at the two flimsy garments which remained between them. His personalised trunks and her flimsy peach silk panties. He smiled, then nodded. 'Why not?' he replied. Then he leapt up from the bed and whipped his own shorts off. He held them out to Amelia who followed suit. Undergarments were exchanged and pretty soon it was all change.

Amelia ran her hands over her hips in their new soft white covering. Not bad. They clung flatteringly to her rounded buttocks and hugged the tops of her pale pink thighs. Guido . . . Well, he looked ridiculous. He stood with his hands held open and gazed at his new outfit with bemusement. The triangle of peachy silk fitted around his buttocks well enough, but at the front he had a lot more than Amelia to hide.

Amelia sniggered behind her hand. She moved towards him and slid her hands over the smooth material, feeling the rough hair beneath. At the front, Guido's penis strained against the skimpy covering, stretching out the little pattern of flowers.

'Just imagine if someone was to take a photo of you now,' she murmured as she placed a hot kiss on his lips. 'Now that really would be something to live down . . .'

Leaving his mouth, Amelia bent her knees and began elegantly to bob down as if she was about to fetch something from beneath the bed.

'No you don't,' he snarled, thinking she was reaching for a camera. Guido snatched for her wrist and dragged her back up again.

'Ow,' Amelia squealed.

'I thought you were getting your camera . . .'

Amelia pulled a hurt face. 'Guido, do you really think that I would be capable of doing something that horrible?'

'These days, I'm just not sure.'

Still holding her by the wrist, he swung her around until she felt the back of her knees make contact with the bed and she crumpled down onto it. Guido followed, landing on top of her. Amelia was about to cry out, but the look in his eyes had changed. They were upturned at the corners. He was smiling. Laughing. Amelia began to laugh nervously too.

'I didn't hurt you, did I?' he asked, sensing that she wasn't quite sure what was going on. Amelia shook her head. 'Can I take these off now?' Guido struggled out of the frilly panties and lay down again, naked. Amelia could feel the sticky head of his penis against the waistband of his shorts and her stomach. She slid her hand between them and gently caressed the hardening shaft with the very tips of her fingers.

'That's nice,' Guido murmured. He shifted very slightly so that she could enclose the whole of his shaft in her hand. As she began to move his foreskin slowly back and forth, he rolled so that he lay to the side of her and propped himself up on one elbow. As she carefully massaged his penis, he walked the fingers of his free hand up the length of her body. He kissed her languidly, enjoying the taste of her make-up as his lips wandered over her face.

Amelia released his penis and took his face in both her hands. She plunged her tongue into his mouth, sucking his own between her lips. Their tongues tangled and wrestled like two fish passing in a stream. Guido moaned and pushed his body closer to hers. Then he fell onto his back and pulled her over on top of him. Amelia found herself astride his loins, his hands on the waistband of his own shorts, which she was still wearing.

He was rolling the waistband down over the gentle curve of her taut, sexy stomach. Amelia helped him ease them off over her legs, then climbed astride him again. It was a very comfortable position that she now found herself in.

Guido reached up a finger and touched it to her lips. Amelia kissed the finger lingeringly, sucking it in between her teeth, nipping it gently. She sat back on her heels and ran her own fingers across Guido's chest. His tiny nipples were erect and he twitched slightly as her fingernails caught the little nubs. Amelia traced the outline of his pectorals, then down across his ribs to the place where his torso split neatly into six tight obliques.

His hands roamed across her thighs, then up towards her breasts, cupping them and squeezing them together. He rolled her nipples between his fingertips, making them stand out red against the pale white flesh. Then he returned his attention to her thighs again, sliding his hands up towards her pubis so that his thumbs touched her labia. Amelia knew she was already wet. He slipped one finger inside her, making her arch her back and smile so widely that she almost had to laugh.

She tensed her thighs and raised herself upwards so that his penis sprang up between them.

'I want you inside me,' she told him hoarsely.

Guido grinned widely and placed his hands on either side of her waist. He lifted her upwards and onto him. For a moment she seemed to hover above his proud, stiff dick. But then she was plunging down, gasping as he penetrated and stretched the longing walls of her vagina. She grasped at his shoulders as she began to ease herself up and down him, the shuddering pleasure in her legs preventing her from being able to go too fast.

'Let's stand up,' Guido said after a while.

Reluctantly Amelia dismounted from Guido's glorious cock and got to her feet. The softness of the mattress made her unsteady.

'Where do you want me to go?' she whispered.

Guido nodded towards the headboard. Dutifully Amelia grasped it with her hands and leaned over. She could feel Guido getting into position behind her. Carefully he pushed her legs a little further apart. She could feel his hand between her legs searching for the opening to her moist desire. The tip of his penis nudged against it. He steadied himself with his hands on her waist and urged himself inside.

Amelia tightened her grip on the tall headboard and drew breath. It was such a fantastic feeling. That sensation of being penetrated. Being stretched. She moaned softly as he began to withdraw. But moments later, she knew, he would be back again.

Guido began to thrust a little faster. Each time he came towards her, Amelia could feel his balls knocking against her pubis, tapping against her clitoris. Intensifying the sensation of each thrust. She tried to reach behind to touch him, but she dare not let go of her support. Instead, she signalled her satisfaction with her moaning.

'That's so good,' she would murmur.

Guido thrust harder. His breath coming in groans.

'Come in me now!' she shrieked all of a sudden. Her orgasm had almost crept up on her. Her pelvis was singing with desire. Vibrating with deep joy. Her nails dug into the wood of the headboard. She repeated her words like a mantra, begging him to come now. To come with her. So that she could feel as if their two bodies were one.

Guido was groaning louder now. Whispering sweet nothings to her in Italian. His grip tightened around her waist. He bashed into her.

She tried to imagine w   nis face would look like. Contorted as it would be by the power of his desire. He leaned forward over her and grabbed for her breasts, which swung down from her body like firm pink balloons. Amelia was coming now, moaning, sighing with the intensity of passion. She could feel her vagina begin to tighten around him. To try to pull him inside. To suck out his come.

Suddenly Guido cried to the sky. Amelia felt his pelvis bump roughly against her bottom. He was coming all over her, deep inside her. Filling her body with his come. At the same time he squeezed at her breasts. Amelia felt as though he was squeezing her whole body. Being with him made her feel so very, very alive.

They collapsed to their knees. Guido was still inside her, so that she seemed to be sitting upon his lap. He pulled her close to him and gave one last orgasmic shudder. Amelia laughed and pulled his cheek towards her. They stayed like that, panting, until their bodies had almost cooled down.

When she awoke the next morning, Guido was still there in Amelia's bed, but this time it wasn't as if he couldn't move if he wanted to. As he slept, he rolled towards Amelia in his dreams and slung a heavy arm across her waist. She tried to move it off again without waking him. He groaned a little as she did so and rolled away, but he didn't open his eyes. Amelia looked as critically as she could at his sleeping profile. His perfect nose. His perfect mouth, lolling open, from which there escaped a tiny snore with every other breath. He was quite the most beautiful man she had ever seen, and last night's events in the light of those photos had shown her that he even had a sense of humour. He would become her steady partner like a shot if she offered him the chance. On paper there was no reason why she shouldn't give him that chance but . . .

Suddenly Amelia remembered waking up alone and upset in Devonfield's bed and realised to her surprise that she wouldn't have minded waking up alone that morning.

Silently she slipped out from beneath the duvet and padded across to the chair upon which her silk wrap was draped like a dead butterfly. She shrugged it on and walked on through to the huge windows of the sitting-room. It was a grey day outside. As grey as that morning in Wales. Now she wished that, like Devonfield, she could leave the room and walk and walk forever too.

Chapter Twenty-One

AFTER BREAKFAST IN her suite, for which Guido did not manage to wake up, Amelia did go out for a walk. She piled her hair into a baseball cap – her own this time – and set off in the direction of Central Park. She got as far as the fence unnoticed. Just one guy had given her a second look while they waited to cross the road, but even that may have been because she attracted his attention when she sneezed. Amelia slipped through the park gates and strode on towards the children's play area. It was a school day and a dull one at that so the park was pretty much empty. She squeezed herself into one of the swings and began to rock herself back and forth like a little girl.

Why couldn't she get that man Devonfield out of her mind? She was a rock star. She could have anyone she wanted and yet the only man she did want didn't even want anything to do with the twentieth century. Amelia closed her eyes and tried to conjure up a picture of his face. His grey eyes with their laughter lines reaching out across his cheeks when she made him smile with some silly joke. His lips, straight and serious but flickering upwards into a grin in the electric moments before he kissed her.

Amelia rocked herself a little harder, until her feet left the ground.

She closed her eyes again and this time remembered his hands. His hands holding hers. Helping her to find the safest path out of his derelict house. Passing her the salt at the kitchen table. His big, strong hands with their long fingers and perfect nails. His firm touch all the way down her shivering back.

He had touched her like a lover.

He had run his hands so slowly down her body. He was like a man who had lost his sight, building up a picture that he wanted to remember forever. She had never felt so cherished, she remembered. No one had ever touched her like that, as if she was more precious than mere flesh and bone. No one. Not before Devonfield and certainly not after.

And his kiss. A thousand of his kisses, all over her body. Sometimes light, like the subtle brush of a petal against her cheek. Sometimes hard, as though he wanted to suck the air out of her lungs. The taste of him. The softness of his lips. The hard sinewy muscle of his tongue, wrestling inside her mouth with her own. His tongue licking her hard. All across her belly. Across her thighs. Right between her legs.

She could feel something within her stirring even at the memory of him. She closed her eyes and she could see the top of his head between her thighs. His hands on her legs, holding them apart. Her clitoris began to throb into life again as she thought of him. He had sucked it through his lips until it was almost between his teeth. She could hear him breathing noisily as he worked at her, until her arousal began to flood out of her. Sweet and sticky, warm and musky. She could taste it on his tongue when he next kissed her on the mouth.

The nerves in her clitoris began to send their messages all over her body. She felt enervated, electrified, to the tips of her fingers as they crept down towards her vagina to complete the circuit. He was kissing her so hungrily then. Kneading her breasts beneath his strong hands, then covering them with kisses. Licking her nipples into greedy little peaks. She arched her back to push them closer to him, closer to his mouth. They were begging for more attention. Her hands moved from her clit to his buttocks, pressing his pelvis down towards her. She was moaning soft encouragement. She gasped with delight as she felt his sticky shaft twitch hard against her thigh.

Amelia dragged herself a little further up the bed. His penis slipped between her thighs, nudging at the place where she was wettest. She guided him towards her deepest core with her hands still on his buttocks. He slipped so easily inside. It was as if they had been designed to fit together. Her vagina, having let him in, tightened around him as if to hold him there forever.

'Oh, yes.' She cupped his head in her hands as he began to move slowly in and out.

Suddenly, the skies opened and began to pour rain down onto the desolate New York park. Amelia lifted her face to the clouds and let the water trickle down her face and across her neck, kissing her, caressing her. The rain seemed like a sign.

She got to her feet and pulled her jacket tight around her neck to keep the water out. But she was much happier now.

She knew she would see Devonfield again. There had to be a way to make him want her like she wanted him.

Chapter Twenty-Two

'DARLING,' SAID ROWENA as they sped towards the penultimate gig in the limo. 'I know that this probably isn't the right time to mention this to you, but you do realise that we're going to have to start working on a new album as soon as this tour is over. As it will be, by the end of tomorrow night.'

Amelia gazed out of the limo window at the buildings passing by. She had heard Rowena, but she didn't answer.

'Have you had any thoughts about it? Things you might like to try? Artists? Producers? New hairstyles?'

Amelia still didn't answer.

'I thought perhaps Freddy Sterling would be an option for you. He's still very hot at the moment. Did the Maraschino Cherries' last album . . .'

'The who?'

'The Maraschino Cherries. You know those boys, they're always being photographed with their clothes off.'

'Oh, them.'

Amelia continued to look out of the window. Three girls in their mid-teens were waiting to cross the road. One of them was wearing a T-shirt bearing Amelia's face.

'We don't have to talk about this now, my dear,' Rowena said after a while, sensing that she was facing a bit of a brick wall. 'But it is something you should give some thought to. We can't use Robin again. He's doing so much coke these days that he doesn't even bother to take the note out of his nose between lines. Just think about your favourites and let me know as soon as you can.'

'I have been thinking about it,' Amelia said as the chauffeur parked the car.

'Oh, good. Well, then. Why didn't you say? Who do you think, babe?'

Amelia swallowed hard. 'What about Tony Devonfield?'

Rowena raised an eyebrow. 'Tony Devonfield? Honey, he would have been wonderful but I don't think he's even alive.'

They walked through the echoing stadium, where the engineers were setting up the gear, to the changing room. Rowena had the key. She opened the door and indicated Amelia's personal space for the next two evenings with her traditional flourish. And as usual, Amelia couldn't see the actual room for the flowers and cuddly toys. She booted a pale lemon llama away to make room for her bag.

'We're going to have to take someone on to deal

with all this stuff,' Rowena told Amelia. 'It's not part of Franklin's job spec to open your presents.'

'Not even if he gets to keep as many as he likes?' Amelia idly picked up a card that was attached to a bunch of pink roses. There were twelve, slightly wilted. 'I love you. Please will you marry me?' said the swirly handwriting in bright red pen. Amelia snorted in amusement. Who was this from? She turned the card over, not really expecting to see a familiar name.

'Bradley Fernshaw, Lubbock, Texas, says he wants to marry me,' she told Rowena.

Rowena was looking at a fax which had just been pressed into her hand by Franklin. It was from the Midnight Records office in London, to let her know that Amelia had just been put forward as a nominee for a Brit Award. 'Everybody wants to marry you, Amelia.' Rowena kissed her charge on the cheek, leaving a little orange circle of lipstick behind. 'Everybody loves you. Look.'

If only that were true.

'This is incredible.' Rowena was reading the fax again. 'Best female artist, best new act . . .' The list of nominations was almost endless. 'You're bound to win something.' Amelia continued to look at her floral tributes in dismay. She picked up another gift card. The writing had been obscured by water dripping from the flowers. But the first two syllables of the name stopped her heart. 'Devon . . . What does that say, Rowena?' she asked desperately.

Rowena glanced from the highly interesting fax to the rather less fascinating card that Amelia had thrust beneath her nose. 'I don't know,' she said. 'It's all smudged.' But seeing Amelia's desperation made her try a little harder. 'I'm not sure . . . but I think it says "Devotion".'

'Not Devon-something?'

'No. Devotion. You got everything you need here for tonight?'

Amelia nodded. She had always had everything she needed. Until now.

Franklin knocked shyly and entered the room again. He dumped another two or three extravagant tropical bouquets by the door.

'Rowena, there's a phone call for you in the office. Some guy says he's a producer and he needs to speak to you urgently about Amelia.'

'Right,' Rowena sneered. 'A producer indeed. These guys will try anything to get through to my precious little star. Franklin, take his number and say I'll call him back when I have a moment. And next time someone calls, remember to ask them their name. How can I decide whether I want to take a call if I don't have a clue who's making it?'

Franklin sloped out of the room again feeling thoroughly told off. Amelia had cleared a space on her dressing-table and was making a start on her make-up.

'All right, toots?' Rowena asked.

Amelia nodded.

'Plenty of lipstick tonight. We're recording for TV. You know where I am if you need me.'

Amelia nodded again.

'Right. I better go and check that I haven't just snubbed someone really special.'

Chapter Twenty-Three

AMELIA DECIDED NOT to bother with the after-show party which was being held to celebrate the end of her most successful tour to date. There would be no one there that she really wanted to talk to. Just journalists, free-loaders and ever-hopeful male models looking for an Amelia-special bondage-break. Since the last time they had met, Guido's modelling career had sky-rocketed and though he would be at the party, he would probably be there with the latest sixteen-year-old sensation from Milan on his arm. Not that Amelia could have cared less any more.

Back at the hotel, Amelia took the lift straight up to her room. Once inside, she kicked off her high patent shoes and padded across the thick carpet in bare feet. She stood in front of the mirror momentarily and looked at her reflection, at the hair cascading around her shoulders and the chocolate satin bodice of her dress, chosen specially because parts of the show were being recorded for TV. A month after going AWOL she was back again. Back in exactly the same position as before. Only this time it was worse.

She poured herself a huge vodka and tonic and loaded it with ice.

And the next day it would start all over again. The recording, the promoting, the touring. Who did she want to produce her next album? Freddy Sterling? Three months stuck in a recording studio with that vertically challenged dope fiend was Amelia's idea of hell. No, she wanted Devonfield. And not just to produce her album.

Amelia sat down at the dressing-table and turned the flower card which Rowena had read as 'Devotion' over and over in her hands. Nothing ventured, she thought. As soon as the airline office was open next morning she would sort out a flight back to London and then she would drive straight from the airport to Wales. She would throw herself on Devonfield's mercy. Tell him the whole story. The worst thing he could do would be to send her away again. Whatever happened, she couldn't possibly feel more loss than she was feeling right now.

Suddenly there was a knock at the door. Very few people could have got as far as the door and, assuming that it was her manager, Amelia didn't bother to answer. The visitor knocked once more. Amelia waited for the sound of retreating footsteps. Rowena probably wanted to know why she wasn't at the party. And she probably had a photographer in tow, or some hack from the local paper. Amelia downed her vodka and poured out another one. She didn't hear the footsteps retreat, but the visitor didn't knock again.

The tape she had stolen from Devonfield was still in her tape player. Amelia switched it on and let the melancholy music fill the room once more. Where was he tonight? Beetling away behind that mixing desk in the middle of nowhere? Searching high and low for the DAT that he had lost? Or perhaps he was staying in London again, calling Sue Lee? Amelia shuddered jealously at the thought. Though it wasn't as if Sue Lee was likely to become emotionally involved with the man of Amelia's dreams.

The knock at the door again.

'Go away!' Amelia screamed this time. 'Can't you understand that I just want to be on my own for a while?'

But the visitor wasn't about to give up now. In the reflection of the room in her mirror, Amelia was sure that she saw the door-knob twist and turn. She swivelled around on her stool. It was definitely moving. Someone was coming in.

'For heaven's sake,' Amelia sighed as the door began to open. 'Can't you just leave me alone?'

'You don't want to become a hermit, do you?'

Amelia's jaw dropped. For there in the doorway was Devonfield. Smiling broadly. His arms loaded with roses. They were even yellow, her favourite colour.

'Can I come in?'

Amelia was already locking the door behind him.

'I can't believe it,' she murmured as he let the roses drop to the floor and she wrapped her arms around his neck. 'What are you doing here?' Then they were kissing, passionately, his mouth roaming all over her face. He seemed to be tasting every square millimetre of her tear-stained skin, as if he was trying to make a map of her with his mouth. Amelia kissed his mouth, his nose, even his eyebrows. Then she pulled away, to check that it really was her man.

'I can't believe it. How did you find out about me?' Amelia asked. 'How did you find me here?'

'Serendipity,' he said.

'What do you mean?'

'Happy coincidences,' Devonfield began. 'And Rowena.'

'Rowena?'

'She put the final piece of the jigsaw in place.'

'After you left,' he continued, 'I went upstairs to work and noticed straightaway that someone had been in my studio. There wasn't quite as much dust as before on the Synclavier,' he smiled. 'I wasn't too worried about it at first but then, horror of horrors, I discovered that I couldn't find the piece I had been working on the day before. Opus Four, the tape I had left out on top. I turned the studio upside down looking for it but I couldn't see it anywhere. I was trying to put the thought that someone had been in the studio out of my mind, but, finally, I had to think the worst of you. You were the only person who had been in the house that day apart from me. And I didn't have a clue who you were or where you would have gone. I called your mobile number and discovered that the phone belonged to a girl called Sue and that she didn't have the faintest idea who you were either.'

'I didn't ever even tell her my name.'

'Now I know who you are, I'm not surprised. Anyway, my last hope of catching up with you lay with the boys from the garage that dragged your car out of the mud. I went down to ask them if they could remember the registration so that I could try and trace you through the rental firm. They didn't have a clue, of course, but it was while I was at the garage that your cover was blown.'

Amelia hugged her knees. 'How?'

'They had a calendar on the wall. And once I had finished flicking through *Exchange and Mart* while I waited to speak to the boss, there was nothing else for me to look at. It was a calendar of 'Babes of the Year' or something like that. Free with some mag. And there you were, Miss February. In glorious Technicolor.'

'How embarrassing.' Amelia put a hand to her hot cheek.

'It still took a while for the penny to drop. I stared at the picture for ages. It was definitely you and I thought that it was possible for a hooker to be a glamour model as well but when I looked at the name beneath the picture, it said that you were a singer. For a while, I thought I must have been mistaken but suddenly it all fell into place. You really were a singer. And certainly no amateur. That's why you were interested in my music. That was why you had stolen the tape.'

'I'm sorry,' Amelia whispered. 'I wouldn't have taken it, but I knew that I wouldn't have time to listen to it before you came back down the hill. I was desperate to hear your work but I didn't know how to ask you. I didn't know where to start. You wouldn't have wanted to play Opus Four to a call-girl.'

'You could have told me the truth.'

'Would you have believed it?'

Devonfield smiled and shook his head. 'But did you like the music?' he asked.

'Very much,' Amelia replied.

'I hope you'll like this better.' He fished in the pocket of his jacket and pulled out another tape. There was nothing written on the insert this time. Amelia quickly ran to her tape deck to put it on. 'It's for you,' he told her as the music began. A piano. Ever so quiet. 'I couldn't stop thinking about you, no matter how hard I tried. Even before I saw the picture in the garage, I hoped that the disappearance of the tape might be an excuse for us to get together again. That night at my house you were so understanding. I felt an instant bond with you that I have never before felt with anyone in my life. For the first time in years, when I watched you driving away from the house, I felt a regret at being all alone out there in my studio and wished that I had asked you to stay. I had been racing back to the house to try to catch you before you left. Didn't you see me?'

'Later, when I found out who you were, I tried to convince myself that you must be some kind of weirdo, a multi-millionairess getting her kicks from pretending to be a working girl and then I thought, perhaps you were just desperate to meet me and could think of no other way, and then I told myself that I was being a stupid arrogant old man. But I couldn't get you out of my head, Amelia. That's when I started to write this piece.'

'I can't ever explain why I did what I did,' Amelia told him. 'It started as some kind of game. But I've been dying to see you again since the moment I left your house. I felt that rapport too but I was terrified that I had imagined it.'

'You didn't.'

'Am I forgiven for stealing the tape?'

Devonfield rose from his hard chair and sat down again on the couch next to Amelia. He touched her face gently with the back of his fingers and smiled. Amelia closed her eyes at his touch and waited for his lips to brush against hers once more. 'I guess you must be,' he whispered as he kissed her.

'I couldn't believe my luck when I finally got through to your manager yesterday afternoon. She said that you had actually asked her if I could produce your next album that very morning but that she told you she thought I was dead.'

'You've certainly been elusive.'

'She had me flown over to see you straightaway.'

Amelia laughed. 'Well, I must remember to thank Rowena for her efficiency, but you realise that she probably expects us to start work on the new songs tomorrow.'

'I don't think we're going to be working for a long while,' Devonfield replied. 'Have I been a stupid fool,' he asked, 'coming all this way to find you?'

'You'd have been a fool not to.'

Amelia melted backwards onto the couch as Devonfield wrapped his arms around her. His tongue, which she had missed so much, parted her lips and probed the inside of her mouth so delicately. He tasted of whisky and cigarette smoke. Amelia sucked his tongue gently but hungrily. She was never going to let him spend so much time away from her again.

'I'm so glad I've found you,' he murmured as he kissed a trail from her throat to her ear. 'I thought about you constantly. Not just because you had the tape, but because of all the things you said that night. You were so different from all the other girls.'

'I probably wasn't being very professional,' Amelia laughed.

'You just need more practice,' Devonfield answered.

His hands moved slowly up the satiny curves of her body, drawing the skirt up her legs as he did so, until the lacy tops of her delicate stockings were visible, with the intricate golden clasps that held them to her suspender belt. Devonfield placed a kiss on the soft bare flesh of her thighs. Amelia felt a flush spread across her whole body.

He was still wearing his tie. Amelia reached for the knot and began to loosen it, until she was able to drag it free. She loosened the top button of his shirt, shivering with the memory of the first time she had done that, reaching across the dinner table to touch him in that peculiar barn in Wales. The dark flash in his eyes when he had looked at her then. The sudden shift in the dynamic as they changed from hooker and client to lovers.

Devonfield's hands were beneath her chocolate silk panties now, massaging the warm willing flesh of her buttocks. Amelia arched upwards in pleasure as she struggled to get the rest of his buttons out of the way. He shrugged off his shirt and his jacket both at the same time and let them fall carelessly to the floor, the one still inside the other. Amelia wriggled until her dress followed suit and Devonfield lay on top of her, his bare flesh against her stomach. She hunted for the carefully concealed fastening on his expensive trousers as he unclasped her bra with one hand, laughing at his own immediate success. The bra joined the dress. Then her panties, floating to the floor as though they were made of feathers.

Amelia heard the clunk of Devonfield's shoes hitting the floor one after the other. He pulled his socks off quickly, nervously, awkwardly, as she simultaneously pushed his trousers down over his hips.

The couch wasn't big enough for them now. Devonfield rolled off Amelia's excited body and onto the floor, pulling her after him. She sat astride him, feeling his erection through his crisp white cotton boxers. Devonfield ran his fingers across her suspenders. She was wearing nothing but her suspenders and stockings now and one by one he flicked the clips open, until the stockings were hanging loose. Amelia kneeled up a little and undid her suspender belt as Devonfield relieved himself of his boxers. The stockings went next, flying across the room like streamers. They were completely naked. Rolling across the floor from the couch to the thick rug in front of the fireplace like a tumbleweed of hot and aching flesh.

When they stopped, Amelia was on the bottom.

They were both panting, both laughing. Devonfield smoothed her hair away from her face and looked deep into the big green eyes.

Suddenly Amelia's face became serious. The smile too melted from Devonfield's face.

'It sounds really stupid but I think that I'm nervous,' Amelia whispered.

'Me, too,' he told her.

'It's not even as if it's the first time we've done this,' Amelia reasoned.

'But it's definitely different now,' Devonfield told her.

Amelia squeezed him affectionately. He buried his face in her shoulder and kissed her white skin tenderly. Amelia breathed in the familiar warm smell of his hair. She let her hands drift downwards over his buttocks. Stroking them. Caressing them. She cupped the firm square muscles and used them to urge his body closer to hers.

Her legs parted around his. She stroked the back of his left calf with her foot. He was still buried in her shoulder. She could feel his breath making her flesh hot. His breathing was ragged. For a moment she was afraid that he might be crying.

'You OK?' she murmured.

'Never been better in my life,' he replied.

Suddenly his face was above hers again. He was smiling broadly. He bent to kiss her and the momentary worries were banished instantly in the contact of their lips.

'I want to make love to you,' he told her quietly.

'I want to make love to you,' she echoed. Her

hand crept down between them then, wrapping itself gently around his erection, guiding it towards her aching centre. She drew her legs up around him and positioned herself to join his body with hers.

'Make love to me now,' she whispered.

Amelia sighed as she felt the first hot inch of his penis slide between her wet and longing lips. Her hands clutched at his buttocks, pulling him further and further into her. Devonfield threw back his head and let out a blissful groan.

'That feels so good,' he breathed.

'So good,' Amelia echoed, holding him there, savouring for a moment the ultimate union of their bodies. Reluctant to let him draw away even for a second.

She wrapped her legs around his back, crossing her ankles. She squeezed his body with her arms and her thighs, feeling his whole body against hers. Feeling closer to this man than she had ever felt to anybody before.

She could hear almost nothing but their breathing, in and out, together, in time. Then the rushing of blood through her ears as she grew more and more aroused. Amelia tightened the muscles of her vagina around his shaft. He sighed gratefully, pushing ever further in. Her pelvis ached with being pushed towards him. Sighing, she let her legs drop away from him, bracing her feet against the floor now, pushing up. Starting the movement they needed.

Devonfield rose above her. An arm to either side of her soft white shoulders. He looked first into her eyes, then down at their bodies. At the point where they joined so comfortably. So naturally. At his strong, hard penis as it slid so easily in and out of her. Each time reappearing more slick than before as they became more and more aroused.

Amelia placed her hands on his waist and gazed up into his face. Each time he sighed with pleasure, she felt her own pleasure intensify. Her enjoyment was so closely tied to his. Each time she cried out with joy, he would push harder. It was an elaborate dance. They were communicating at the ultimate level. Knowing without words what to do next.

'You . . . feel . . . so . . . good,' he told her. A word for each time he entered her. He placed a hand beneath the small of her back to protect her from the hard floor and to lift her pelvis higher so that he could drive deeper. She pushed down through her legs to help him on.

'Deeper, deeper,' Amelia moaned, wanting more and more of him inside her still. His hairy balls tapped against her perineum, intensifying the sensation. Her fingernails dug into the firm, twin cheeks of his bum as they tensed and relaxed, tensed and relaxed. Each time he plunged into Amelia, he let out a small, animal-like grunt of pleasure, which transferred that pleasure to her. They became faster and faster, a grunt for each thrust, a thrust for each beat of her heart until suddenly the rapid thrusts became one long plunge. Devonfield held himself in position against Amelia's body, raised on his arms, his head thrown back, his mouth open, gasping for air, as his loins twitched convulsively.

Amelia pushed up against him, willing this climax to continue forever, as she shuddered with the joy of fulfilled desire and he flooded her with hot sticky come.

Afterwards they had rolled apart and were lying on different sides of the rug but their hands were still touching. Their fingers entwined. Amelia gazed at the ceiling, tracing the intricate plasterwork pattern with her eyes. From the sound of his breathing, she could tell that Devonfield was falling asleep. The combination of excitement and jet-lag, she smiled. With an enormous sigh he rolled towards her until his head rested on his shoulder. It was heavy, but Amelia didn't mind. She didn't mind anything that night.

Chapter Twenty-Four

THE NEXT MORNING Rowena almost choked on her muesli when Amelia announced over breakfast that Tony Devonfield would be the producer of her next album after all, saving her actual choking for the subsequent announcement that Amelia was also going to become his wife. They were going to fly back to England for the wedding as soon as they could get booked onto a flight and would start work on the new album right after the honeymoon. Amelia would have to telephone Karis first of course, since as Amelia's best friend she would have to be the maid of honour. But this time, Amelia smiled to herself, no messing about. There would have to be a proper hen night.

New *X Rated* titles from *X Libris:*

PRIVATE ACT
Zara Devereux

Kasia Lyndon is a good-looking but struggling young actress who is thrilled to get her first break at the Craven Playhouse, a privately owned theatre company in a country manor house.

But this is no ordinary theatre, and she must live her role both on and off stage – even when it demands that she submits herself to her sadistic leading man and his mistress. Kasia, however, soon discovers that this domination has unleashed feelings in her that she never dreamt she had.

0 7515 2739 4

THE DOMINATRIX
Emma Allan

Karen Masters has never been very interested in sex. But when she sees a video of her friend Barbara engaging in some very *outré* sex games with her husband Dan, she begins to realise what she has been missing.

Beautiful redhead Pamela Stern is a dominatrix and more than willing to show Karen exactly what this means. As she wields the whip Karen's sexuality comes alive, and when she discovers that one of Pamela's clients is her own boss Malcolm Travers, she agrees to become his personal dominatrix. Now Karen can fully explore the limits of her own desires, at least until Malcolm's wife finds out . . .

0 7515 2976 1

G-Strings

THE X LIBRIS READERS SURVEY

We hope you will take a moment to fill out this questionnaire and tell us more about what you want to read – and how we can provide it!

1. About you . . .

A) Male   Female

B) Under 21   41-50
    21-30   51 -60
    31-40   Over 60

C) Occupation_____

D) Annual household income:
    under £10,000   £31-40,000
    £11-20,000   £41-50,000
    £21-30,000   Over £50,000

E) At what age did you leave full-time education?

    16 or younger   20 or older
    17-19   still in education

2. About X Libris . . .

A) How did you acquire this book?

    I bought it myself
    I borrowed/found it
    Someone else bought it for me

B) How did you find out about X Libris books?

    in a shop
    in a magazine
    other _____

C) Please tick any statements you agree with:

    I would feel more comfortable about buying X Libris books if the covers were less explicit

    I wish the covers of X Libris books were more explicit

    I think X Libris covers are just right

    If you could design your own X Libris cover, how would it look?

D) Do you read X Libris books in public places (for example, on trains, at bus stops, etc.)?

    Yes   No

3. About this book . . .
A) Do you think this book has:

Too much sex?
Not enough?
It's about right?

B) Do you think the writing in this book is:

Too unreal/escapist?
Too everyday?
About right?

C) Do you find the story in this book:

Too complicated?
Too boring/simple?
About right?

D) How many X Libris books have you read?

If you have a favourite X Libris book, what is its title?

Why do you like it so much?

4. Your ideal X Libris book . . .
A) Using a scale from 1 (lowest) to 5 (highest), please rate the following
   possible settings for an X Libris book:

Roman/Medieval/Barbarian
Elizabethan/Renaissance/Restoration
Victorian/Edwardian
The Jazz Age (1920s & 30s)
Present day
Future
Other

B) Using the same scale of 1 to 5, please rate the following sexual
   possibilities for an X Libris book:

Submissive male/dominant female
Submissive female/dominant male
Lesbian sex
Gay male sex
Bondage/fetishism
Romantic love
Experimental sex (for example, anal/watersports/sex toys)
Group sex

C) Using the same scale of 1 to 5, please rate the following writing styles you
   might find in an X Libris book:

Realistic, down to earth, a true-to-life situation
Fantasy, escapist, but just possible
Completely unreal, out of bounds, dreamlike

D) From whose viewpoint would you prefer your ideal X Libris book to be written?

Main male characters
Main female characters
Both

E) What would your ideal X Libris heroine be like?

Dominant	Shy
Extroverted	Glamorous
Independent	Bisexual
Adventurous	Naïve
Intellectual	Kinky
Professional	Introverted
Successful	Ordinary
Other	

F) What would your ideal X Libris hero be like?

Caring	Athletic
Cruel	Sophisticated
Debonair	Retiring
Naïve	Outdoors type
Intellectual	Rugged
Professional	Kinky
Romantic	Hunky
Successful	Effeminate
Ordinary	Executive type
Sexually dominant	Sexually submissive
Other	

G) Is there one particular setting or subject matter that your ideal X Libris book would contain?

H) Please feel free to tell us about anything else you like/dislike about X Libris if we haven't asked you.

Thank you for taking the time to tell us what you think about X Libris. Please tear this questionnaire out of the book now and post it back to us:

X Libris
Little, Brown
Brettenham House
Lancaster Place
London WC2E 7EN

Other X-rated fiction, available by mail: